WHEN THE FIRE STARTED

WHEN THE FIRE STARTED

A Historical Novel

MELISSA E. DUGAN

When the Fire Started

For information about this title or to order other books and/or electronic media, contact the publisher:

Melissa Dugan
Melissadugan10@gmail.com
MelissaEDugan.com

ISBNs:
979-8-9892779-0-2 (softcover)
979-8-9892779-1-9 (eBook)

Printed in the United States of America

Cover and Interior design: 1106 Design

All scripture is taken from the New International Version of the bible.

Words have power; they can set a people free,
or enslave them.

Acknowledgments

First, I want to thank Robyn Groth. It was in her writer's group that I came to see my strengths and weaknesses. Then her challenge was: move on.

I owe a great deal to Ron Adkins. He was my encouragement at a low point and a great help as content editor.

With his technical expertise, Cyprian Alexzander made the way a great deal easier.

And of course, my husband Rodney Dugan, my chief encourager.

How we need our community!

Contents

Prologue

Some say the storm started in 1517 with German priest and theologian Martin Luther's revolution. It came to be called the Protestant Reformation. Before Luther printed his "95 Theses" attacking the corruption of the Church, most Europeans were Catholic. Within twenty years, much of the continent belonged to the Reformed, or Protestant church as Luther's preachings spread throughout Europe. Upheaval continued to move across Europe as peasants, complaining of their mistreatment of over-taxation and confiscation of their land, went to war against their overlords. Peasant leaders justified their actions using some of Luther's arguments. He had encouraged people to read the bible for themselves and through that he gave the common man and woman power over their lives. The peasant wars, which began in Germany, spread to Switzerland as did Luther's influence on the reformers. And the troubles broadened. In Zurich, Switzerland, the reformers had taken control of the city from the Catholics, who had armies poised in Austria to take the power back.

Into this turmoil came a small group who disagreed with the reformers and with the Catholics. They wanted their freedom, and this is their story.

Chapter 1

Zurich, Switzerland, Fall of 1524

The morning light bathed the herb-drying room, reminding Priscilla that she was late. She stood looking at her hanging herbs. *Did she have everything she needed? Yes, she did.* She took her shawl from the peg on the wall, placed her large basket filled with herbs and tinctures into the crock of her arm, and opened her home's ornately carved wooden door. Stepping onto the stoop, she glanced up the cobblestone street, and her heart sank. It was that judgmental, harsh neighbor. She didn't feel like facing her this morning. Priscilla stopped, frantically wondering how to avoid her. Then, seeing it was inevitable, she took a deep breath and continued down the steps, expecting to meet the woman at the gate.

At that moment, her neighbor Bella waved to her and shouted, "Priscilla, let's walk together to market." Priscilla felt a sense of relief at evading the likely confrontation. The woman passed by, glancing her way with a sour look. Priscilla nodded toward her but wasn't acknowledged. By then Bella stood before her, bringing her sunny disposition. Priscilla felt rescued.

"That neighbor from up the street," Bella whispered as watched the woman pass by, "she's so stern." Bella turned toward Priscilla, puzzled. "She seemed awfully angry as she looked at you."

Priscilla, not wanting to delve more deeply into the situation, answered, "Let's keep moving. We don't want to miss the best of the market."

"Oh yes, yes, of course." Bella caught up with Priscilla. Breathing deeply, she focused on the basket and said, "Are you carrying herbs?" she inquired, prying a bit.

"Yes, I am attending someone after the market," Priscilla answered with reserve.

"Oh, I thought you no longer practiced using herbs."

Priscilla redirected Bella's attention. "Do you think Hans will be at the market today?" she said.

"He generally is."

"Do you appreciate his goods? "Priscilla said, adjusting the basket on her arm.

"I do, indeed. His meat is the best."

"I agree. I hope he will have a goose for me today." Priscilla picked up her pace and said, "If we don't hurry, the best produce might be gone."

As they walked along, Priscilla greeted others she knew with a nod. She was long and lithe with a regal way about her and was well respected by many in the city as the daughter of the Master of the Weaver's Guild.

Bella chatted as they walked, quieting as they approached the clamor of the market. The two paused to observe the market's raucous activity. Priscilla enjoyed the energy there, the vendors calling out to the passersby. Many were peasants from the countryside surrounding the city. She imagined they were pleased and proud to present the efforts of their hard work.

Bella looked confused. She pointed. "Where is Hans? Doesn't he usually take that spot?"

"There he is. I see his table," Priscilla said. The women started that way.

As they drew near, Bella said, "Hans, we looked for you in your old spot."

"I like to keep my buyers on their toes," Hans said in his young and energetic way.

"Oh Hans, you have made it difficult for your best customers. That would be Priscilla and me," Bella said, equally playfully.

"Well then, welcome ladies," he said with a slight bow. "What can I do for you today?"

Priscilla said, "I am looking for a goose."

"Good choice, ma'am, good choice. Did you want a live bird or one I have prepared?"

"One you have readied."

Looking over his fowls, he chose one, and handed it to her. "Yes ma'am," he said. "Here you are, for you and the master's meal tonight."

The bird was plump and beautiful, just as she expected from Hans. She thanked him for it.

Their purchases complete, the two explored other vendors' wares. They chatted with other merchants and enjoyed browsing and buying. When she was satisfied with her purchases, Priscilla leaned toward Bella and said, "Well neighbor, I must part ways with you here. I need to be on with my morning."

"And you must take the herbs to someone you will be treating?" Bella said, prying again. "Well, you have always been very talented as an herbalist. Everyone says so. And as a midwife."

"I no longer do midwifery," Priscilla said abruptly.

"Oh, I didn't know. That's too bad," Bella said quickly, looking puzzled.

"I will see you later in the week." Priscilla hurried on, happy to avoid any more of Bella's questions. She planned to walk past the grand cathedral, the Gross Muenster, walk over the river, and visit the home of her friend Katrina and her family to administer the herbs.

As she passed down the familiar street, she heard a commotion in the distance. Approaching the old church, she saw people gathered around the steps. This was not unusual; people often preached to the crowds there. She needed to get to Katrina's, but she felt drawn to the gathering, and her curiosity won out.

It was a large crowd. She moved toward its center, fighting the push of it and attempting to look over heads, hoping to see more.

She stopped to ask someone, "What is going on? Why are so many gathered?"

"It's a peasant speaking against the landowners."

She knew peasants gathered there often to talk about the injustices they were experiencing. Unbearable taxes and landowners seizing their fields were some of the many wrongs against them. She agreed with the peasants' concerns but wondered at the wisdom of confrontation. She was rarely confrontational.

At that moment two men rushed by her, one nearly knocking her over. Looking up, she saw him stop and look back at her. Recognizing her, his expression changed from annoyance to anger. She stared at him. He stared back and then turned away.

This stirred up long-buried memories, leaving her shaken. She felt the pain of those memories. Yet something within her pressed her on to see what the commotion was about. She continued moving through the crowd, determined to get to the source of the trouble.

Reaching the front, she realized the person preaching wasn't a peasant after all. It was Felix Manz, a member of her faith community and a friend. Moving closer, she saw what was happening. Standing in front of Felix in a threatening way were three council members; one was the man who had passed her. She tried to listen, but the noise of the crowd prevented her from understanding what was being said. Now she saw the councilmen roughly push her friend, and her heart felt bruised for Felix.

One of the peasants began yelling, "Leave him alone."

Another one close by said, "He should have the freedom to speak in the square!"

And another, pointing to the church behind the crowd said, "He makes more sense than what is said in this cathedral."

Just then, Felix looked at her. She nodded to him and he to her. The councilman who had jostled her saw their exchange and regarded her with disdain. Seeing this, Felix began speaking over the heads of the councilmen standing in front of him. With his strong, compelling voice he addressed the peasants assembled, stirring the crowd even more. As Priscilla watched, one of the councilmen pushed Felix, and, to her horror, Felix forcefully pushed him back.

What now? she thought. If only she could help him, but what could she do? Felix nodded to her as if to say he was all right. She felt the freedom to leave and hurried off.

Dear God, she prayed earnestly, *please protect Felix*. She rushed down the street toward Katrina's, shaking inside. Wanting to put the incident out of her mind, she began to consider the herbs she had chosen for her friend. She felt certain the combination would have the desired effect to cure her friend's fever. Because of their poverty, life was a struggle for Katrina's family. Priscilla wanted an end to this added burden of sickness. She thought of her precious friend and how some in the city might criticize her friendship with a peasant family. She was well aware that the Anabaptists', as they were called by others, values were not widely understood. Perhaps they would never be.

Priscilla knocked at Katrina's door. The oldest daughter, Margaret, answered. Ushering her in with urgency, Margaret said, "Priscilla, I am glad to see you. My mother has never been this sick before. Usually, she doctors herself with remedies, and then she's better."

"Please lead the way, child."

Walking through the humble family area, Priscilla noted two of Margaret's brothers playing a game on the floor. She watched them laughing and this lightened her mood a bit. She was grateful for the distraction; focusing on her fear and guilt at being unable to help Felix wouldn't be good at this time of healing.

Margaret led her into the small bedroom, where there was barely enough room for the two of them to stand around the bed. Priscilla paused to observe Katrina's eyes, skin color, and general appearance. At that assessment, she gained confidence in her choice of herbs.

"How are you feeling, dear one?"

"Tired and discouraged. There's much to be done here in the house." Katrina looked around then asked Priscilla, "What do you have for me, friend?"

"I've brought two herbs for you: pennyroyal and burdock." Priscilla took them from her bag. "Have you used them?"

Katrina nodded, saying she was familiar with them and had used them before. "Did you go to the market today? Was Hans there with his delicious meats?" Katrina asked, apparently wishing for the normalcy of the day-to-day life she knew before she was sick.

"Hans was there doing brisk business as usual. The market was fine; it was what happened on my way here that was disturbing."

Katrina looked concerned. "Whatever do you mean?"

"As I passed near the old cathedral, I saw Felix preaching on the steps. This, of course, is nothing new. The young men seem to spend many mornings there lately. The disturbing part was how some of the councilmen there treated him in a most disrespectful way—to the point of pushing him."

Katrina gasped. "I wouldn't expect that from them."

"I was surprised and alarmed. It made Felix angry." She sighed and looked down. "I felt bad that I couldn't help him."

"What could one woman do in that case?" Katrina asked weakly.

"The crowd was his protector, I suppose. I think the councilmen were afraid of them. The peasants were adamant that Felix was being misused. They made it clear that the council was acting unjustly. I'm concerned about what this will mean for our community." The last part she said as if thinking out loud. Then, regretting her words, Priscilla patted her friend's arm, "You need to concentrate on getting better and I need to get going."

Katrina called to Margaret, "Come daughter, show Priscilla out."

On her way out, Priscilla walked through the family area. She noticed Margaret wearing a tattered apron meant for a larger person, one with flour spilled down the front. She wondered how the twelve-year-old was coping, having to take her mother's place. The brothers were still playing their game, laughing and giggling. As she came near, they stopped and looked up innocently.

Margaret glared at them. "Boys, you have work to do. Now get to it." Margaret said this in a stern voice, one she had probably heard her mother use. Once Priscilla and Margaret moved through the door, the giggling started again. Priscilla thought again of Margaret taking on this responsibility so young.

Standing outside, Margaret looked at her pleadingly. "Will my mother get better?"

"I believe she will. God has given us herbs for our healing. We will trust in Him."

Margaret smiled and seemed comforted.

"Here's your job, Margaret: You need to be strong for her. Sit by her bed and speak words of love, healing, and encouragement. If you do this, after a time, she will become your encourager again." Priscilla smiled at her and said, "Good day now. I have to hurry on." She picked up her basket, left, and started up the street toward home.

As she neared the Gross Muenster, she felt the tension she had experienced earlier. The crowds were gone, as she had expected, but her fear remained. Stopping where she had stood earlier, she was surprised that the feeling became more intense. As she walked up the hill to the shelter of her home, her only thought was she must talk to her father about this.

Chapter 2

Priscilla shut the big wooden door behind her and leaned against it for a moment. She wanted to shut out the memory of the morning's violence against her friend. Most of all, she wanted to shut out her fear. She had thought if she could just get to the warmth of the home she loved she would be safe. But the fear remained. What would the incident mean for their community? Her body tensed, and tears pooled in her eyes. She shook her head. *Enough of this!* She must prepare for the meal and meeting tonight, and later tell the others the story. She placed the basket on the table and entered her herb-drying room to retrieve herbs for the meal.

She heard Greta, the new cook, enter the house to start her day. Priscilla called out, "Greta, I have a goose for you from the market."

"Yes, ma'am. Was the market busy today?"

"Very busy," Priscilla said as she walked into the kitchen where Greta stood. She reached into the basket to retrieve the fowl. "I'm turning it over to your capable hands." Priscilla smiled at her. "Please prepare it with these herbs," she said, laying them on the table. "And cook the stew slowly."

Greta gave a slight curtsy. "Yes, ma'am."

"There will be five of us tonight. And will you make the same cake you made last week . . . and bread, of course?"

"Yes, ma'am."

As Greta worked in the kitchen, Priscilla sat nearby, hoping her father would come home early as he did at times. After a while, thinking over the morning's event, she knew she must leave to find him. "Greta, I'll be back later." Before Greta could reply, she was out the door and headed for the weaver's guild, where she expected her father would be.

Priscilla entered the large front room of the guild hall and listened to the rhythmic sounds of the looms at work. She stood for a while, thinking of how she liked the smells and sounds of fiber being fashioned into the fabric on the looms. Although she had come with a string of emotions in her heart, she couldn't help stopping to admire the finished goods produced by the apprentices and touching the newly loomed work. It thrilled her when they worked with silk and linen. Their luxury was like none other. She wondered which overlord had commissioned such fine and expensive fabric. Taking one more quick glance around the room, she knew she needed to get on with her business.

Moving toward one of the weavers she stopped to comment. "Samuel, I see you are progressing nicely with your skills. Will you be moving on to the position of journeyman soon?"

"Yes I will, thanks to your father. He is a good teacher, one of the best. I am thankful to be in the guild. I am but a peasant," he said humbly.

"You are very talented, Samuel. I hope you know that." Priscilla nodded to the young man dressed as many of the peasants did in simple pants and a jerkin. She hoped he understood she wanted to honor him.

He looked down, his face red. "Thank you." Looking up, he said, "Will you be continuing your weaving, ma'am?"

"Yes, I miss it and am anxious to get back to it."

At that moment the guild overseer walked through. "Michael," she called, "could I have a word?"

"Yes, ma'am?"

"I was wondering, where would I find my father?"

"You just missed him. I believe he went to talk to someone about a new project."

"Oh, of course, the tapestry. Thank you, Michael."

As Priscilla made her way home, she considered the evening to come. There was much to do to prepare and ready the house. She had hoped to speak to her father about what would surely come up in conversation. Perhaps it was best this way; she would have time to take a breath and get ahold of her emotions. The proper time would present itself later. As she considered the day's events again, she felt a new emotion arise. Along with fear, there was anger. Was it necessary for Felix to stir up this trouble?

Then, for some reason, she thought of her husband, who had been taken from her some years earlier by sickness. If only she had him again to comfort her. She sighed, thinking a husband and marriage were not for her now that she was in her forties.

❧

Jakob strode down the cobblestones, acknowledging those he met on the way. He was tall and dignified with kind eyes that had seen much in his sixty years and were now weary. His white hair was ordinarily kept tidy, but today it was a bit disheveled by the wind. He wasn't bothered; he had other things on his mind. What should he do about the work that had been commissioned by the overlord? Perhaps he could negotiate with him to depict another subject.

At that moment, he heard his name called. He looked up to see the very man he was thinking of standing before him.

"Good day, Master Jakob," the landlord said in a stiff, formal way.

"Good day, friend," Jakob answered in his measured way, as if he weighed every word. "I was just thinking of you. You must come by the guild tomorrow and we will talk about your piece."

"Yes, tomorrow it will be." After some further conversation, the landlord moved on.

Making his way down the street, Jakob pondered the scene the man wanted: Swiss soldiers on the battlefield, fighting against the Holy Roman Empire, something in which there remained a great deal of pride in Switzerland. But Jakob was a pacifist, and his views on war were not understood. As he walked, he brooded over the many changes in the last year—disturbing and confusing changes. If only the Brotherhood could go back to what it had been before: shared hearts and shared lives, quietly meeting together and no one seeming to take notice. Now it seemed they shared only uncertainty. *We are not a people who meet in towering edifices, led by men in flowing robes. We are people with a simple faith, those who gather in homes to share each other's lives, sitting around tables with our bibles open. We worship simply and humbly. Rituals have very little meaning to us. That's who we are.*

He remembered how high expectations were when Huldrich Zwingli, the pastor of the Gross Muenster and a great orator, took control of the city council nearly a year ago. They had thought there would be freedom for their beliefs. The Protestant reformers seemed to be in one accord with them. At least that's what was said in the beginning. *Perhaps a new war was brewing, one not to be fought on the battlefield. How does a man of peace resolve these things?* It was a question Jakob asked but he wasn't certain there was an answer.

As he turned the corner, Father Thomas's house lay ahead. They disagreed on matters of faith, but Jakob was always welcomed there. The housekeeper greeted him at the door and ushered Jakob into the opulent home.

The priest said, "Welcome, my old friend to my humble home."

They walked to the sitting room where some of the tapestries Jakob had made in years past greeted him. He took a moment to enjoy them as old friends. Knowing the priest wanted a tapestry larger than what he had previously purchased, Jakob wondered what the response would be when he quoted him the price. Very few in the canton of Zurich could afford such a thing,

Father Thomas broke into his thoughts. "So, you have come to talk about the tapestry I have in mind?"

"Yes, tell me of your plans."

They walked into another part of the house.

"I would like it to hang just there, with the others I have in the hall. What I see is a flock of birds flying over a serene lake, trees in the background, perhaps waving a bit in the wind. I would like it to be set in the fall to take in the color," the priest said as they stood looking down the hall.

Jakob took in the space again. He wanted to carefully observe the colors and the designs of the other pieces and note the light in the area. With that, he became excited about the possibility of stitching such a large and challenging project.

Turning toward the priest, Jakob said, "I have some ideas for a tapestry that would go well with the others. Let my assistant and I discuss this, and we will prepare a sketch for you. How does that sound?"

The priest agreed. Gesturing toward a chair, he said, "Please sit with me for a time."

Jakob sat, hoping Father Thomas didn't want to discuss matters of faith. He didn't care for contentious disagreements.

"Are you comfortable? Would you like a glass of wine?"

"No . . . no thank you," Jakob answered politely, wondering why the priest never remembered that he didn't drink.

They talked for some time as old friends about the local news and people they knew. Then the canon stopped talking. He looked at Jakob and said, "We were young together. Remember, Jakob?"

"Yes, a very long time ago. As I remember, we were wastrels," Jakob answered thoughtfully.

"I suppose we were," the priest said with a bit of a smile. He paused, then said, "Jakob, how is it I never see you at my church? You would make a good Catholic."

"Friend, you know our differences."

"Of course, of course. You never follow up on my invitation, do you? Well, I will look forward to the finished tapestry."

After leaving, Jakob reflected on his times spent with Father Thomas. There was often a sense of pressure to join a side, to choose between the Catholics and the Reformers. His group had no intention of choosing either side. They were the Brotherhood. They had quietly existed for many generations alongside the dominant church. They were people lost to history. And for many years their consciences had spoken to them of another way. And to that way, they had listened.

Chapter 3

Tall and handsome with a touch of gray, William, one of the council members, watched anxiously from the back row of the chamber as the council assembled. He kept his eye on the door, noting the mood of the members as they entered. Some were agitated. They whispered among themselves, angry for having been called away from their work. He chose to sit apart in the back, but he stood, as did the others, when the newly appointed broad-shouldered and commanding magistrate, Bruno Heinrich, entered and the meeting started.

The magistrate spoke brusquely: "Why have we been called here today? What is our business?"

The three councilmen from that morning stepped forward. The oldest spoke. "It's the Anabaptists. One was preaching in front of the old church. Something must be done."

The room broke out in raucous grumblings. Some whispered, "The heretics!" Others complained, "Must we be bothered by this today?"

The magistrate yelled, "Quiet!" Once the crowd complied, he said harshly, "Does this man have a name?"

"Felix Manz."

"Yes, and we know him well, don't we? This is not the first time he has caused trouble in the city. Please give the assembly more information. Some of you engaged him?"

"He verbally abused us. And he pushed me."

"He pushed a councilmember! Please take note, all," the magistrate said, outraged.

"And he was stirring up the peasants against us."

"This cannot be tolerated. We have standards and laws in this city and in the canton of Zurich. Now these fools stir up the peasants with their idiotic ideas. It's shameful how they teach against the baptism of babies. This has been the norm for untold years," he said. "Our traditions hold us together," he added, as if to remind himself. He gestured toward those attending. "Infant baptism has been in place before any of you were born. It is paramount. Our babies, all the babies of the city, must be baptized. Now this group comes against it. *It is shameful. It is nonsense. And I will not have it*!" He glared at the three. "Why didn't you bring him in?"

"The crowd was unruly. The recent peasant war came to mind," the tallest councilman replied.

"So, he was stirring up the people? That could have had a serious outcome." The magistrate thought for a moment, his expression darkening. "This is the group led by Jakob, the master of the weaver's guild? Why isn't he taking control of his group? He is a member of this council, although not active of late. Perhaps he should be censured and disciplined. As guild master, there should be some retribution."

All agreed, except a lone voice in the back row.

William stood up. "Sir, I want to say something."

"Yes, William, you have the floor."

"Should not we consider the reputation of Jakob before censuring? As the master of the weaver's guild, he and his work are well respected in the city. He trained my son, who is now in a successful, prosperous business. Should these things not be considered?"

The magistrate stared at William with scorn. "The accusations against Jakob are serious. Do you side with this group, William?"

William hesitated.

"Well then, sit down." The magistrate went on with the meeting.

William sat but thought that at least he had spoken up for Jakob. He had to defend his honorable friend whom he had always admired. Yet part of him saw their point: faith and the council had always been one. In years past, the Catholics controlled the council. But then, in 1523, Huldrich Zwingli won control for the Protestant reformers. William asked himself: does the alliance of faith and the state hold us together, as we have been told? His thoughts troubled him. *What to do?* His loyalty to Jakob was unbreakable. On the other hand, maybe he was being foolish and in danger of damaging his position with the council. He had to think this through.

The magistrate's voice broke into his thoughts. "We will have to consult with Zwingli on this. Let's put this off for another day. This meeting is adjourned."

Priscilla sat on the stool near the large open fireplace, encouraging the flames with a poker. She considered how this ordinary day had changed so dramatically. With the fire attended to, she got up, stretched her back, and moved toward the window, thinking, *Papa, please come home or there won't be time to talk before the others come.* She sighed and turned her attention to preparations for the evening. She set the table using her best dishes. Then she went to the window to watch for their friends, Felix Manz, Conrad Grebel, and Conrad's wife, Barbara. They would break bread and remember the Lord tonight. She looked forward to these times of sharing scripture and the Lord's table. Their homes were havens protecting them from those who disagreed with their beliefs. Some even called them heretics. This thought weighed heavily on her mind. She thought about how unjustly Felix had been treated and wondered what her father would think.

Her worries were interrupted by wonderful smells wafting from the kitchen in the next room. Her stomach growled, and she remembered she hadn't eaten since early morning. Greta would work out well if these mouth-watering smells were an indication of future meals.

She went into the kitchen. "What do you think, Greta? Has your stew turned out as you hoped?"

"Yes ma'am, and all the more thanks to your herbs. I am very happy with it."

"And the bread?"

"It will be ready for the guests."

"And I thought I saw some cake set out earlier?"

"Yes. Just as you like it, ma'am."

"Our guests will arrive soon. Thank you for your excellent effort."

Priscilla felt a sense of relief. The meal would be as she had planned. She wanted this to be a time of comfort and encouragement for the others. The day had been one of adversity; tonight would center around comradery and sharing.

A knock came at the door. She opened it to see Felix arriving early. He greeted her warmly, as always, but she could see a heaviness about him. "Let's sit in the other room," she said. "Sit there in my father's chair near the fire. Warm yourself, the season is changing with the fall chill."

Priscilla watched as Felix rubbed his hands before the fire. "I am glad you are the first to arrive, Felix." She scanned his face, trying to discern how he was fairing. "How are you doing? It was shocking to see how you were treated this morning." She was careful to avoid bringing up his response. "Did the councilmen surprise you with their actions?"

"I'm still mulling over the morning. It could have had a more dire end," Felix said.

"What do you mean?" she said with concern.

"I responded in a less than respectful way, didn't I? Which I highly regret. I suppose the surprise was that I wasn't taken in to see the magistrate."

"Perhaps they feared the crowd."

"I think that was the key."

"When my father arrives, we can discuss it more." Priscilla decided not to start the conversation about the morning's events at dinner. She would wait patiently, but what sat on her heart was nothing like patience.

Another knock came at the door, and Greta ushered Conrad and Barbara into the sitting room. Felix rose to greet them. Then they sat, enjoying one another's company until at last Jakob burst through the door.

"Please forgive my being late, friends. Is it time to eat?" he asked Priscilla.

She hastened into the kitchen to alert Greta. Back in the dining area, everyone was settled around the table. Greta brought in the food, and Priscilla helped serve. She wondered if others felt the anxiety she did. Then Felix began to speak. Priscilla's tension mounted as she imagined what would come forth.

"Jakob, have you heard what happened this morning as I preached on the steps of the old church?"

Jakob shook his head. "No, was there a problem?"

"Not until I began to preach on infant baptism; how it's not in scripture."

"I see. Go on."

"Lately I've noticed the councilmen in the crowd, simply observing. But when the subject of baptism came up, that's when the trouble started. They began to yell at me."

Jakob looked saddened. "We agree with the council on many things regarding faith. It is a shame that a ritual should bring division between us. We should be brothers, the council, and our group. Baptism at birth or choose it as an adult; that's our disagreement, is it not? Perhaps I will have to have a conversation with them."

Priscilla looked at Conrad. He seemed different tonight. She saw something in his face, an unexpected hesitation. She would ask Barbara about it later.

After the meal, it was time to remember the Lord and His sacrifice for them. Priscilla and Barbara cleared the table to prepare for this time of sharing. From the kitchen, Priscilla brought the chalice filled with fragrant juice made from grapes she grew in her garden. Barbara followed her with a loaf of bread on an old plate used for years for what they called the Lord's table. The women sat.

As the meeting was held in Jakob's home, it was customary that he take the place as leader for the night. After some scripture, Jakob said, "Let us now partake of the reminders of the body and blood of Christ that was shed for each of us." They each broke off a piece of bread from the loaf, dipped it in the juice, and celebrated communion together.

Afterward, they sat quietly, and Priscilla felt the presence of the Lord as she often did in their gatherings. Opening her eyes, she glanced toward her father and saw his serenity. But neither Felix nor Conrad seemed to share that tranquility. She felt their distress tonight. Felix's story was fresh in her mind but Conrad's mood continued to be a puzzle.

Jakob's eyes were closed as he quietly waited. They all joined him in waiting on the Lord. During this part of the meeting, they trusted that someone in the group would have a scripture or song to share but tonight nothing was said.

Jakob waited a bit longer, then opened an eye to look out over the group. Priscilla saw that he shared her puzzlement. Then he opened both eyes and said, "First chapter of John, verse four says: . . . 'for everyone born of God overcomes the world. This is the victory that has overcome the world, even our faith.' This is the scripture that has been on my heart today. Does anyone have a comment?"

He looked at the group, Felix and Conrad in particular, still wondering at their mood. After a time, he shrugged his shoulders and said, "Barbara, would you have a song for us tonight?"

Seemingly pulled out of a malaise, Barbara said, "Yes, there is a song I've been thinking of. We haven't sung it in a long while. Do you remember, 'Majestic Lord'?"

The suggestion lightened the mood. Jakob said, "Yes, that's perfect. Lead out, Barbara and we will follow you." After the song, they stood. Holding hands, they shared more prayer together, the women first and then the men.

When they finished, Priscilla said to Barbara, "Let's you and I clean the table and help Greta set the kitchen right. Then we will have some of her wonderful cake."

In the kitchen, Greta was setting the cake on plates. When she left to serve the others, Priscilla turned to Barbara. "I have noted something in the face of your husband that I haven't seen before. How is he responding to the news of Felix and the council?"

"He is apprehensive about the turn of events and has much concern for the welfare of our good friend, Felix. But there are complications in this matter."

"Complications?"

"After this disturbance between the council members and Felix, some members went back to the council. Together they have been putting pressure on Conrad's father, demanding that he take his son under his control." Barbara paused. "His father is a council member, I'm sure you know that."

Priscilla nodded.

"Well, his father came to our door this afternoon, as angry as I have ever seen him, his face red and swollen. He came in and began to berate Conrad, saying he had been a disappointment for years and had brought disgrace and shame on the family with his association with the Anabaptists, as they are calling us lately. Then he brought up Conrad's attack against the church taxing the citizens of the city, which, of course, we don't want to pay," she said, looking earnestly at Priscilla. "We don't want to pay for a church system we don't support and aren't a part of. His father went on and on about it."

Priscilla noted the tears forming in Barbara's eyes. "That must be very hard on you, friend."

"I am concerned for Conrad. He loves his father so." She paused. "And the baby is coming soon," she said, placing her hand on her growing belly and rubbing it, as if to comfort her yet-to-be-born little one.

Priscilla placed her arm around her friend's shoulder. Barbara smiled and went on, "Conrad wonders if Zwingli has encouraged this upsurge in attacks. Zwingli says Conrad has betrayed the gospel. They were friends at one time." Priscilla heard the emotion in her voice and nodded for her to continue. "It's good to be able to share my heart with you, Priscilla. You are a good friend." Priscilla squeezed her shoulder and gave Barbara a kiss on her cheek.

Soon after this, Conrad and Barbara left, leaving Felix. Priscilla knew he had more to say. The three sat around the fireplace and Jakob, perched on the three-legged stool, stoked the fire. When he had brought it up to a good warmth, he returned to his chair. They sat together in silence as was their custom. It was a form of prayer, quietly listening to God.

Jakob started the conversation with, "Brother, you have something on your heart."

Looking at them with the same expression Priscilla had seen earlier, Felix said, "I didn't want to share this around the table, because I didn't want to add to Conrad's burden, and also," he hesitated, "I'm not sure I wanted them to know all that I experienced this morning. I wondered if they would think less of me if they knew I had lost my temper."

"I see, go on," Jakob said sympathetically.

Felix looked into the fire. "For the first time I was afraid, Jakob. I feared what they might do to us. In the past, there have been many threats, but I didn't take them seriously. Today was different. I have never seen such hate in the councilman's eyes, in his face. And it's what he said, Jakob."

"Yes."

"He said, 'You will live to regret this, Felix Manz. You and your Brotherhood.'" Felix paused, with a look that seemed to Priscilla to be very vulnerable. She remembered how young he was, only twenty-five. Today he looked younger, and her mother's heart was stirred.

With his usual sagacity, Jakob asked, "Felix, are you certain that public preaching is what you are called to do?"

"I am assured that it is my calling. I have a fire here." He pointed to his chest.

"Well, then, you know what you have to do."

After Felix left, Priscilla said, "Papa, what do you think the magistrate meant by saying Felix would live to regret it?" Something within her shuddered at the unknown.

"We will see, daughter, we will see. I have an idea. Let's take up our instruments and play a bit tonight. We need the calming."

Priscilla agreed. She took up her flute and began a piece of music they hadn't played for a long time. It was sweet and tranquil. Then her father joined in with the lute and they were taken to a place where music reigns. And for a time, nothing else mattered.

Priscilla glanced at her father. "Papa, what are you thinking?"

"Your mother—I was thinking how beautiful she was." After this, they were lost, each in their own memories. Jakob continued, "When she picked up her instrument, she could take me to another place, it was almost another world."

"Yes, I remember it well. I loved her music also. Did you know when I was little, I would hide at the top of the stairs to listen?"

"Yes, I saw you there, attempting to hide," he said with a twinkle in his eye.

"Papa, when I was a child, I thought you and Mama were the originators of music and that it flowed from you like the streams that flow out of the mountains into the rivers."

Her father laughed. "Ah, the thoughts of a child."

"I have another memory of that time. I remember one night when I had fallen asleep at the top of the steps. Mama carried me to bed whispering, 'This is not for little ears.' That's when I first discovered the secret meetings, when you and the others gathered for music, to pray, and to read the old spirituals. I heard the men spiritedly debating, and one or two women joining in, with more measured tones. It piqued my curiosity, I wondered, *What is this?*"

"Yes, those days long ago." he said, barely above a whisper, "She was so beautiful and now she is gone. I miss her so."

They both returned to their thoughts, Jakob missing his wife and Priscilla remembering her mother and missing her also.

After a time, Jakob came out of his reverie. "I saw the priest today," he said, "and we discussed his new tapestry."

"Yes, I know. I went to the guild looking for you."

"The priest is an old friend from my youth. I was a prodigal when I was young." He stopped for a moment, hoping not to shock his daughter. "I don't think I have ever told you this about myself. My parents were people of faith, part of the Brotherhood, but I wanted nothing to do with it. I would go to mass because I loved the music there. Afterward, I would meet Thomas, before he was a priest, of course. He and I would drink too much, then walk through the city full of drink, singing songs that belonged to the world. I'm not proud of it now. I was a rebel against my parents and their faith. And yet, there was for me a drawing toward that faith.

"It wasn't until I met your mother and observed her life and her heart that things began to change. She started me on a new path. She was good and I admired her beautiful soul. And the music, it drew us together. It drew me to her and, as a result, to God. There were times when I felt I was carried to the Holy Spirit on the notes of her flute. How could there not be a God of wonders when I knew and felt the music like I did? And how could I not be drawn to Him when I thought there was a bit of God in the beauty of music? Later I found, of course, music was only a taste of the Lord, only a beginning."

He chuckled. "I came to know He was so much bigger. I found life in Christ and then my world opened. I found a world I didn't know existed. After that I joined the Brotherhood. And now I trust God won't remember the sins of my youth, as the scripture says."

Priscilla noticed her father's hands, as he gestured, were becoming ever more wrinkled. He was getting older. But he still had a regal way about him.

"Bedtime, daughter."

"It has been quite a day."

"Tomorrow will be better," Jakob said firmly.

"I hope so," she said, apprehension in her voice. "I hope so!"

Chapter 4

Lord of all tranquility
O incline to us thine ear

Priscilla picked up a loaf of bread at the vendor's table, adding it to the basket on her arm. As she did this, her eyes rested on a young woman next to her wearing a blue shawl. Without speaking, without words, a knowing look passed between them. *What was it?* she thought. Just as quickly the thought was gone, and she moved on with her day. As she approached Hans's table, the young woman passed by, looking over at Priscilla again. Priscilla nodded but wasn't sure the woman had seen her because she didn't respond.

Hans noticed. "She's a sad one, isn't she, ma'am?"

"Yes, I agree," Priscilla said as she watched the young woman walk away. "Does she come here often?"

"Yes, she does." Changing the subject, he asked, "What are you looking for today?"

She went about her other duties then headed for Katrina's. Walking the cobblestone street, she crossed the bridge over the river Limmat and considered her interaction with the young woman. Something about her seemed familiar. Hans was right, she did seem sad and alone, set apart from others. Priscilla decided to watch for her the next time she went to market.

Margaret greeted her at the door. "Good to see you, sister. Mother is better, it looks to me."

"That's what I wanted to hear." Priscilla handed Margaret her shawl. Walking into the next room, she was happy to see Margaret's observations proved correct. She took a moment to assess Katrina's condition. Her friend looked healthier. Her skin color and her eyes looked better, and today she was sitting up at the table.

Priscilla sat down across from Katrina. "I feel you are much improved. You are not completely healed, but I had expected it would take more time. I've brought herbs to add to what you are taking. I believe in a week to ten days you will be good as new."

"Thank you, dear friend! You are very skilled at treating with herbs. Do you have a great many different remedies?"

"I have an entire room filled with the fragrance of many herbs," Priscilla said with a smile.

"I have seen your large garden."

"It is my delight. I look forward every year to the task of caring for it. I will have to close it down soon with the coming change in the season, and I will miss it."

"I also have herbs drying, enough to take care of the common ailments of my family. But you are the master. And you are a midwife also?" Katrina added.

"No, I don't midwife anymore. Are you back to cooking for the family?"

"A little. Margaret does most of it. She has been very sweet to me lately. When she has time, among her many new tasks, she will sit by my bed, and hold my hand. She tells me what is going on in her heart. Other times she will read scripture to me. I am very glad of this; I feared she didn't believe." She continued, "It's been a time of turning toward each other. Our relationship has been uncomfortable lately. But now I think we are past that," she said, smiling weakly.

"I am very glad," Priscilla said. She stood. "I'm afraid I must go now. I expect to see your bright smile the next time I visit. I hope and will pray for your complete healing."

❧

Jakob sat at his loom, considering the piece he was working on. But in truth, his thoughts were in a far different place. He was remembering how the Brotherhood had had a measure of peace with the prior magistrate and the council. Things had changed. He wondered if it was because of the new magistrate. He considered this sadly. *Bruno is a sterile, stiff, proud man,* Jakob thought. He sat before his forgotten work thinking about a dream he'd recently had about Bruno. He'd seen the magistrate as a giant bird flying about the city, searching for those who didn't obey him. Jakob watched him swoop down to take his prey in his giant talons, carrying them off to be punished. It was unsettling to have someone sitting in this place enforcing the law when their Brotherhood could be possible prey. Today he determined to talk to this man with the perpetual scowl. It was Jakob's obligation to see this out—no matter the cost. But what might that mean to their group? What about the guild he had worked so hard to build over the years? Nonetheless, he decided, reluctantly, to meet Bruno this afternoon.

&

"Why are Anabaptists troubling the council? What will you gain by this, Master Jakob? You are dividing the city."

Jakob studied the magistrate sitting before him. When Bruno entered the room, he sat, but he didn't offer the same to Jakob. Jakob stood, observing this man with the same severe face he had seen in the past. Now he used the name Anabaptists, meaning rebaptizers. Jakob supposed the magistrate could call them whatever he wanted. They didn't have an official name. They simply called themselves the Brotherhood or the brethren.

The magistrate continued, complaining, "The young men preach in front of the old church against our commands."

Several times, Jakob attempted to interject but was cut off. Finally, the magistrate paused from his rant. Jakob said, "If I may speak?"

"Yes, have your say," the magistrate said gruffly.

"We hoped that this body of city leaders, as a part of the reform movement, would take time to examine our beliefs." Jakob paused, looking thoughtfully into the magistrate's face, and wondered, *Is he listening, really listening?* Taking a deep breath, Jakob continued, "Our main contention, of course, is your demand that our group have our babies baptized by the reformed church. This goes against our beliefs, convictions, and principles. We look to the bible as a guide for our lives and for our faith. The holy scripture makes no mention of the baptism of babies." Jakob sighed deeply. "Rather, baptism is offered to adults when they have come to a place of personal belief in the Lord as savior."

The magistrate broke in and countered with, "Yes and those beliefs do not line up with what has been established here in this council. As you know, our people have controlled the city government for the last year, having taken it over from the Catholics." He raised his voice. "And your group does not honor our position that all the newborns in the city must be baptized!"

Jakob listened patiently, only somewhat aware of what was being said. He wondered how long he would keep his place on the council as master of the guild after this conversation. Then he thought about the other reasons the magistrate was responding so harshly toward their faith community. He felt events from the past had colored the magistrate's opinions. Soon, the meeting ended abruptly, and he walked home with a heavy heart.

Later that day at home, Jakob sat leaning forward, his face in his hands, considering how poorly the meeting had gone. He blamed himself. If only he had made a stronger case for their beliefs. Disappointment hit him like a fist to the stomach. It hurt deeply to be rejected by those who had been friends, those who had respected him and his place in the community. But he could and would bear it.

Arriving at the guild, he scanned the room. All were at their proper places, heads down, deep in their work. He was grateful to not be noticed as he strode to the back room where he could have privacy with his work and his thoughts. No one to bother him there with questions, inquiries, and problems. He wanted solitude to think. He sat at the loom weaving, wondering at how this work soothed him. It was like the effect the music had on him. Perhaps it was the rhythm of it. He worked and he prayed. And after a time, his sorrow was forgotten.

❧

Chapter 5

The young woman in the blue shawl knelt in the back of the old church, in the midst of the battle—wrestling with her inner argument. Anna's head was bowed low as she knelt in the darkness. She wanted to hide from God. Considering her life these days, she was certain He must want to punish her. Yet she had questions. Should she hide from Him or seek Him out? And if she sought Him, where might she find Him? That was what had brought her to the Catholic church. Surely He would be in this beautiful place. She admired the altar, the stained-glass windows, and the wonderful paintings. She thought this church must be a favorite of His.

Then she was drawn back to the pain in her heart. As she dwelt on the unrest that raged there, she didn't notice a man's entrance. Then she heard him. Looking up, she saw him moving with resolution, like a silent force, his large wooden rosary beads rhythmically tapping and bobbing at his side.

She froze. It was a monk! Did he know her secret? Anna stared as he made his way to the front of the church, kneeling under the large crucifix, then prostrating himself face down on the floor. She shuddered; she would never go that close to God. Wouldn't He condemn her?

Anna sat transfixed, suspended in the moment. Just when she felt she must escape, the monk cried out with sobs of pain. She couldn't understand his words, but she felt them. She knew that emotion, that pain. His prayer was her prayer. Listening closer, she realized he was speaking Latin, so she began adding her own words, her own cry. This was a fellow sufferer. His pain was deep, and she knew that language. "*Mea culpa, Mea culpa*, my fault," he said. "*Mea maxima culpa*, my most grievous fault."

She joined his litany and was caught up in it, repeating the phrases over and over with her head down. She looked up and then, just as suddenly as he'd come, he was gone. For a moment she wondered if he had been real. Perhaps this was a vision. Or maybe it wasn't. She knew she had to leave.

Later that day, as Anna treaded the familiar streets toward the market, she pondered the monk. Why was he so troubled? What was his life like in the monastery? She thought the monks didn't have the same freedoms as the parish priests, and she mused on how his life might differ from Father Fredrik's, her parish priest.

"It's funny how I still call him Father considering—" Her thoughts trailed off. "Yes," she said to herself with sadness, "it is sort of funny."

She realized she must hurry. Today was bread-making day and she needed to buy the ingredients—yeast and a few other things—and head home to the rectory. Breadmaking was her greatest talent; all the visitors to the rectory commented on the quality of it. She felt pride in that. She loved the entire process: the kneading, getting the oven just right, and the wonderful smells at the end. There was much joy in it. Anna walked toward the market, hearing the usual cries of the vendors hawking their wares. Some were amusing, some droll, each with a message. She passed by the first table quickly. She could never remember the fishmonger's name, or possibly she wanted to forget it, as his fish always smelled poorly. He should take lessons from Hans on how to sell, she thought.

Anna was just one of many picking up what they needed for the day. They were women like her who worked for others. A few tables up she found the needed ingredients and filled her basket.

After finishing her tasks, she headed for the rectory and came upon a man preaching to a crowd about his differences with the reformed church. They seemed a regular presence these days. She made a mental note to stop and listen closely the next time she passed one. She would tell Fredrik what she'd heard. She thought about how he hated them. *The Protestant reformers are troublemakers*, he would say.

Rushing now, because it was getting late, she glanced at a house she had always admired and saw a kitten she had seen there before. Today she couldn't resist. Carefully, she moved closer. Then, stooping down, she picked it up. It peered at her with earnest eyes that seemed to be saying, *Take me with you, please.*

"I can't, little darling. Fredrik would be furious with me," she whispered to it. Stroking it lovingly, she set it next to a building where she thought it would be safe. "Maybe someone will be kind and take you in."

She turned and started on her way. Then, for no good reason, she looked up and saw a bird of prey flying overhead. It was beginning a dive toward the kitten, its talons out. She ran back and dove for the helpless little one who had only her as its savior. She grabbed it, put it in her basket, and rushed away. The kitten went limp after its near calamity. But within minutes, it gave a whimper and poked its head out of the basket with a meow. She felt a sense of relief. *It would be all right.* She forgot about the market, the preacher, and all that had happened. Impulsively, she headed for home with no thought of the outcome of bringing this little orphan to a place where it wouldn't be welcome.

At the rectory, she took the kitten to her small room on the second floor. She cradled the little one like a baby. It willingly played its part, purring as it lay in her arms. "You have called to your mother and siblings but there was no answer," she whispered. "I am your family now. You have been longing for a home, haven't you? I know, I have been watching you. Now you have one, here with me." The kitten purred and Anna smiled at it. She felt the kitten understood her and she it. For a moment she thought about how alone she had been feeling. No mother, no father, and no children. It was the last part that was the most painful. No children . . .

❧

Would they be watching for him here? Maybe it was a mistake to come to the market. Remy, with his young, tortured eyes, slowed his pace. The pain was more intense today, sharper than before. He rubbed his leg. It wasn't healed yet, but he had to keep moving. He was angry and cursed quietly. He heard the sounds of the market ahead and hoped Hans would be there. He needed him to be there.

Hans had his back turned, arranging his meats nicely to draw the next buyer, unaware of Remy behind him. Remy paused to watch his brother, hoping for the answer he needed. Finally, he spoke up: "Hans."

Hearing the familiar voice, Hans turned quickly. "Remy!" Looking him over, head to foot, he said, "You look terrible. Are you all right? We haven't seen you for months. Are you still a part of the canton's army, still fighting to defeat the overlords?"

"It's too long of a story. Hans, can you give me some money?"

"You know I can't do that; our father watches the purse too closely. Stop by later and I'll give you some food."

"Oh yes, father. Maybe I don't care what father thinks," Remy said under his breath. "Sure, sure. Whatever you say," he said aloud bitterly.

"Stop back when the market closes and I'll have something for you," Hans said, concern in his voice.

❧

Busying herself around the sitting room, Priscilla found some dust, cleaned it off, and stood by the window next to her father.

"Did you see her, Priscilla?" Jakob said, turning toward her.

"Who?"

"The young woman. She rescued the kitten we have been watching for days."

"Rescued it?" she said, distracted as she adjusted the curtains.

"Yes, just as a large bird dove for it, hoping to make it a meal for tonight. She grabbed it and put it in her basket. I'm glad about it, aren't you?"

Priscilla said, "Oh yes, that poor little thing. We watched it struggling for days. You put something out for it to eat." She looked out the window and saw the young woman, the one from the market with the blue shawl and big sad eyes. She saw her hurrying away with the rescued kitten.

❧

Why didn't Hans just give me the money? Remy asked himself. *Oh, I know. Hans is the good son. And then there is me. Maybe father is right, I'll never amount to anything. Isn't that what he has said?* Then he thought, *I shouldn't have come to the city. They are probably looking for me here. I've got to keep moving.*

A stabbing pain coursed through his leg. He cried out with a curse. He slowed and leaned against a tree. Then he heard a kitten's cry and saw a young woman save it from a bird of prey. He thought, *At least someone cares for those in need.* Bitterness and bile flowed through him. He had to get out of the city. Someone from the army might see him.

Remy walked on. He stopped at an unattended fire at the edge of the city. He hoped for just a moment to be able to enjoy the warmth. He squatted there, focusing on his problems, his face mirroring his thoughts with a scowl, as a man approached him.

"Who are you? And what are you doing here?"

He made no answer, not looking at the man.

"You better move on."

Remy stood painfully. "Move on . . . to where?" he said and limped away. He started out of the walled city, moving north into the woods. He wanted to find a place under a tree to rest, to sleep. He needed sleep badly, and a place where no one would bother him, a refuge from the cold. Maybe a tree that would welcome him. Exhausted and wincing from the shooting pain in his leg, he found a large pine tree surrounded by a comfortable bed of pine needles accumulated over many years. It was ready to comfort a tired wayfarer. Remy laid down his few belongings with a weary sigh and ate the ham and pottage Hans had given him. He hoped, by some act of God, tomorrow would be a better day. He had no plans. More to the point, no dreams for the future. After the food was mostly gone, he wrapped himself in his cloak and curled up under the pine, hoping for a peaceful, if not a warm sleep. He was drifting off, almost at the stage of a dream when he heard a strange sound like that of bits of wood bobbing in the wind. Remy sat up, fully alert now. "Who goes there!"

"It's me, Strong Jorg."

"Show yourself—friend or foe."

"I'm not a foe to anyone, at least not to most. I could ask the same of you. And you are sleeping in my place!"

Remy was surprised at the large man he saw before him. He said, "You wear the robes of a cleric. What are you doing out here?"

"Same as you, I guess. I'm sleeping in the woods. And a very pleasant place it is, except for the fact it's getting colder, and you are still in my spot," the big man said more impatiently.

Remy grudgingly moved. As he did, the monk noticed his leg. With more compassion, he said, "What happened to you? You're in pain."

"I've just left the canton's militia. I was wounded in battle." It was a lie, but he said it anyway.

"The peasants war?"

"Yes, I am myself a peasant. I fought alongside my oath brothers. We were one and with one cause," he said proudly.

"The peasant wars, will they be won?"

Remy's face darkened. He said bitterly, "I don't know. Who does?"

❧

Chapter 6

Perched comfortably on a chair, Anna peered over the book she was reading, scanning the library. The first time she entered it she had been enthralled. She had been a child then. She had no idea there were that many books in all the world. This library had opened much to her. As she set her mind again on the book before her, she was startled by a voice from the doorway.

"What are you doing in the library? Isn't there work to be done in the house?"

She breathed out heavily, realizing Fredrik had been drinking again. "I've been reading some of Martin Luther's writing . . ."

"Why would you do that? Now tell me, why?"

She was afraid of Fredrik when he was like this, so she spoke swiftly to try to assuage his anger. "It's just that I was at the market, the preachers talked of Luther, and I was curious. I heard you mention him, and I thought we could talk."

"Those preachers are fools. All of them. I hate their arrogant ideas. First the Protestant reformers in Germany, now Zwingli here in the city, and now these other idiots, the Anabaptists. You stay away from them. Do you hear? There is plenty to do here in the house."

She bore his anger as she had in the past. Remembering what had worked before she began speaking in soft tones to him. This soothed and quieted him. Finally, he said, "You should go now to your work."

As she walked toward the library door, he said, "Wait. Do you know anything about the cat in my stable?"

Before she could think of how to avoid answering, Fredrik spoke with resignation, "I have that small shed now when once I had a fine house with a fine stable and more horses than I needed. I was forced to move by those Protestant reformers. No respect for my position, no respect for me. I don't like this change and now there's a cat I can't catch."

He was quiet for a time. Then he walked up to her, took her hand and said tenderly, "You understand, don't you, Anna? You are always patient with me." He looked into her eyes, leaned over, and whispered in her ear, "Join me tonight, after you have finished your work."

Priscilla, wanting to get an early start for the market, took up her basket and left the house. She paused as she often did to admire the view of the mountain peaks to the east with the mist lingering over them. Approaching the market, she noticed the vendors were moving faster today with the changing season. Pulling her shawl closer around her shoulders, she felt a change—something beyond the changing of the season.

Nearing Hans, she asked about the day's offerings. Feeling someone behind her, she turned to see the woman with the sad eyes and was surprised when the woman spoke to her.

"Ma'am, haven't I seen you in the crowd, listening to the two men preaching? The heretics they call them." Anna stopped, unsure of herself. "Weren't you there?"

"Yes, I was, yesterday," Priscilla said with caution. *Can I trust this person?* she thought. There was such uncertainty lately.

"I have questions. Could we talk about what was said? I need to know more. My name is Anna, by the way."

Priscilla saw her earnestness. She said, "Of course, let's walk. My name is Priscilla."

Anna had many questions about faith. Priscilla did her best to answer them. As they neared her home, she pointed it out. "That's our home. We sometimes have meetings there. Please feel free to join us tomorrow night at the guild hall, if you like. We would enjoy your presence. All are welcome, and you can learn more about us and our ways."

❧

The sun had come out from its hiding place behind the clouds with the goal of warming the city, but Anna didn't notice. She walked with her head down, pondering her conversation with this new friend. She had much to think over. She decided she would attend the meeting. It would be dark tomorrow night. That would be good; no one would see her enter the guild hall. Fear ran up her back. How should she feel about attending a meeting of those called heretics? She must conquer that fear. She had to know more about these people who were so passionate about their beliefs and their God. Perhaps they had something she was looking for.

Felix and Conrad stopped at their usual spot to preach and read new broadsides to the people in the square. Felix was the first one to notice him. He leaned over to Conrad, "Do you see him?"

"Who?"

"The councilman with the long beard. He's watching us."

Conrad surveyed the crowd. When he saw the councilmember, he said anxiously, "Should we turn back? Perhaps we should not proceed with our plans."

"No! Today we will be as bold as lions, brother. Our mission is a righteous one and we will not be thwarted or turned away from it."

Yes, this is a new day, Conrad thought. He was energized and encouraged by his friend at his side, and he felt an old fire returning. Looking over the crowd again he remembered that councilman as a thorn in the flesh after Conrad criticized the Protestant church for leveling taxes on the people of Zurich. He had paid heavily for that stance and had been publicly shamed, which caused more problems with his father.

The two watched as a good-sized crowd formed. That's what they were waiting for. Felix strode purposefully up the church steps. He turned toward the crowd saying, "People of

Zurich, listen! I have a message that needs to be heard!" He glanced at Conrad.

Conrad called out to him, "Our mission is a righteous one. We are bold as lions!"

Felix could understand only part of what Conrad said because of the noise of the crowd, but he understood Conrad's intent. Encouraged, Felix looked over the eager crowd and read from the broadside he held. "There are those who would silence a message, those who will not listen to the voice of the people." The crowd called out their affirmation. "This is the message being silenced. Salvation is in Christ alone. Baptism doesn't save. Rather, salvation comes from the moving of the spirit on the heart of the individual. Salvation comes when a person believes, when they enter into faith in the Lord Jesus." He added with passion, "The baptism of babies is therefore wrong and goes against the teaching of the bible."

The councilman yelled from the crowd, "You men, stop now!" He advanced toward the preachers. "By what authority do you speak?"

Felix leaned toward Conrad and said, "Now, a little friendly debate." Conrad nodded, feeling more confident.

"Again, by what power and authority do you speak here?" the councilman shouted as he came closer. "We alone have the power and authority in this city to regulate religious speech. You are not Zwingli men. Therefore, from this time forward you are forbidden to speak in the square or anywhere publicly in the city. Now leave before we take you in."

Felix and Conrad looked at each other, knowing they would obey God rather than man. And that they would be back. They walked briskly, trying to put as much distance between them and the councilman as possible. As they walked toward Conrad's home, they vented about the council's interruption.

"He said we weren't Zwingli men," Conrad complained. "Although we were at one time."

"Aye. We spent hours under his teaching, and we learned a great deal about the bible and faith. There was much agreement amongst us."

"Agreed, but then he changed. He said the church could not be independent of the local government. That's when we parted ways. Now we are looked upon as enemies by those we once held in deep regard," Conrad said sadly.

"Yes, but we will carry on. We must. We are called to it."

That night, many of the brethren were gathered at the guild hall. Glancing around, Priscilla felt the excitement in the room. Leaning toward her father who sat in front of her she said, "The young men are rising up. They are full of fire, Papa. They aren't holding back. You should have seen Felix preaching with conviction. I suppose that means we are no longer hidden as we have been in the past. It's not possible now with the young men's fervor. They are strong pillars and witnesses for the Savior." Priscilla paused, remembering Felix and Conrad's speeches that morning. "I was proud of them for how they stood up to the councilman. He was very angry." Her father nodded. She leaned back and noticed Anna. Anna's eyes shone with the same life that Priscilla felt in the room.

Felix and Conrad spoke proudly of their victories, the numbers that had gathered when they preached, and how many people asked questions and told of their changed lives. The two spoke with bravado, talking of how things would change in the city, how they had won over many of the peasants. And how they thought that eventually, the council would bow to their demands.

Priscilla noted that her father was silent, with a far-away look. She planned to ask him later what he was thinking.

At home, Priscilla and Jakob settled into their comfortable chairs. Still cold from the walk home, Priscilla sat near the fire, rubbing her hands together to warm them. She continued to feel the animation and excitement from the meeting, so she chatted on about how she had felt earlier watching the men preach. Finally, it occurred to her that her father wasn't responding. He had the same serious expression she had noticed at the meeting.

"What did you think about the meeting tonight, Papa?"

"The young men don't know the history of those who have believed as we do."

"What do you mean?"

"They don't know what those who went before us experienced: the harsh reality of those in the past who have gone against the dominant religion. The history of the church has been one that was hard on those who dissent; first it was the

Catholics and now the reformers. The brothers don't know where this path will likely lead."

Now, fear took the place of excitement in Priscilla's heart, and she shivered.

Chapter 7

Tired and feeling broken, Fredrik slumped into his chair. He had started drinking early in the afternoon.

"That stupid cat. How is it a creature that small can avoid capture by someone my size?" he slurred. But the cat wasn't the problem, it was his unresolved business. He had gotten word that his father had died suddenly, and it stirred rage in him. Now his drinking had the goal of drowning memories and missed opportunities. He sat in his big chair in the library thinking about his overbearing father, falling in and out of a wine-induced sleep.

Waking, he muttered, "It wasn't my choice . . . the restrictions . . . I must have a woman in my bed." He looked toward the door of the library. "Where is Anna?" He stumbled out of the room and went to look for her.

The cook is gone, no need to keep our secret tonight, Anna thought as she lay next to Fredrik, who was staring at the ceiling. *He is so handsome with his dark eyes, jet black curly hair, and his charming ways.*

He looked her way. "I didn't want to become a priest, you know." He was thoughtful and talkative tonight and a bit drunk. She had heard the story before, but she listened patiently.

"My father forced me into the priesthood. He thought it would cure my waywardness. He was a hard man, my father, and one to whom it was impossible to say no. So here I am, playing a part. The parish priest. Ha! I'm not happy." He rolled over to look at Anna. "I suppose it's not entirely true. Being with you gives me moments of happiness." He took her hand and kissed it. "Do you love me, Anna?" He put his arms around her and pulled her close. In that moment there was a melting in her heart, and she forgave him, saying, "I do love you, Fredrik."

Then they heard an unexpected noise in the house. "Should I leave now?"

"Yes. I will see you in the morning. Just be quiet on the steps, I think the cook may have come home earlier than expected." She looked at him anxiously and left his bed.

The next morning, Anna made her way down the creaky steps, considering her duties of the day. One would be bread-making, her favorite job. She walked into the kitchen and passed the cook, who swiftly turned from the small stove and grabbed Anna's arm.

"You went to bed very late last night," the cook said, squeezing Anna's arm roughly, hurting her.

In a panic, she searched for a believable excuse. "I was in Father Fredrik's library. I like to read—"

"I heard him tell you to stay out of his library."

"I waited until he went to bed."

"Oh, I see you know his habits. When he's asleep, and when he's awake?" the cook said accusingly. She dropped Anna's bruised arm, stared at her for a time, then turned away in disgust.

Anna knew that now the cook would hate her. The cook's attitude did change. She ordered Anna to do rougher work and criticized and complained about her at every turn. And she said that Anna could no longer make the bread.

Anna endured this treatment for weeks. Then it came to her: maybe if she appealed to Fredrik, he would advocate for her. She went to him when the cook was out.

"What do you expect me to do? Let her go?" Fredrik said.

She shook her head. "No, just talk to her. She will listen to you as her employer."

"I can't risk losing her. She is a very fine cook, the best I've ever had. She is the sister of my friend, and it would be an insult to him."

"I could cook. Then we could be alone. No one to bother us."

He laughed. "No, that's not going to work. She'll get over it. You'll see."

Anna felt abandoned. She had been certain he would stand up for her . . . or had hoped he would.

Later that day, she went about her work dusting in the big library, moving more slowly than necessary. She hoped the cook wasn't watching closely or she would surely receive a reprimand from her. Anna was moving the books and dusting around them, stopping to investigate some that she was interested in reading. She was so deep in her thoughts, she didn't notice when Fredrik entered the room, quietly shutting the door behind him. He approached her from behind, put his arms around her waist, and kissed her neck. She froze, not knowing what to expect. She had mixed feelings about her situation. Today, she felt trapped.

"Come to me tonight."

She agreed, only because she hadn't been given a choice. She was coming to understand that in her life she had no choices. Again, a heavy sense of guilt overtook her. What should she do?

Later that afternoon, when she had a spare moment and knew no one was looking, she went to her sparse room and shut the door. She knelt by her bed and looked up at the crucifix on the wall and the small picture of St. Agnes that hung near it. She had been praying to St. Agnes because she knew the saint had been badly treated by men. Anna felt St. Agnes would understand her need. But then she looked yearningly at the cross. Maybe she would pray to Jesus. Yes, that's what she would do. He would answer her need. She felt certain He would be her rescuer.

That evening, when she and Fredrik were together, she watched him as he lay on his back, deep in thought. She had to ask him now. She needed to know the answer. "Fredrik." she took a deep breath in and asked, with something of a child's heart, "Do you love me?" There was no response. Fredrik just lay there. Then he got up, dressed, and left the room. She sat on the side of the bed and looked at the crucifix on the wall above the bed. The thought came to her again, *What should I do, Lord?*

❧

Priscilla sat on the stool before the half-finished tapestry that would eventually go to the priest. She mulled over the problems she faced with it. *Those birds, she just couldn't get them right.* She had made attempt after attempt, and she was getting frustrated. She took out some of the stitches she had placed the day before. As she did, she decided to step back from the piece to get a different perspective. She moved from the stool and walked to the back of the room to look at it from there. Maybe she would see something she hadn't noticed before. In doing that, she began to reflect on how this work brought such immense satisfaction to her. The colors, the textures, the landscapes, and what the scenes spoke of—stories of those who had gone before and the lives that were commemorated. It was all a treasured part of her life, and she was happy that she could experience it and be a part of the guild.

She recalled how, when she was a young girl, her father had called her to his workplace. Having seen some of her sketches, he had recognized her abilities. She had been drawing for years. Now he saw, with training, she could progress to another level and be useful at the guild. When she had grown more and her size allowed it, she was given projects to complete on the loom. She became a weaver. Eventually, he invited her to join him at the guild. She was proud to be one of the very few women allowed to be part of the weaver's guild.

Her eye was drawn back to the tapestry. She stood with her hand under her chin, brooding over her work. *The birds flying over the lake toward the woods in the background; the scene wasn't working. What could she do to fix it?* She moved back to her stool, contemplating her dilemma. Her father strode over to stand beside her, gazing at the piece.

"Is there a problem? Do you need help?" he asked.

She said, "It's what I told you about days ago, Papa. I can't get the birds to match the picture I see in my mind's eye. I am attempting to capture depth here, so the birds seemed to be farther away. Do you have ideas for me?" Her father had given her time to figure it out for herself as he always did, and she appreciated his patience with her. But now, despite her determination to come to her own solution, she realized she needed help.

"I think it has to do with the scale and size of the birds. Why don't you do this with the wings?" Picking up a pen, he sketched his ideas on a nearby piece of fabric. "Have one bird with the wing turn this way. And with the other two, weave the wings differently, like this. What do you think, daughter?"

"That is a perfect solution!" She leaned toward him to give him a kiss on his cheek.

"I'm proud of you, daughter. Have I told you that lately? You are very skilled."

Priscilla smiled at Jakob. "Thank you, Papa."

"I thought of something as I walked to the guild this morning."

"Yes, and what was that?"

"I thought of your poetry. I don't see it anymore. It always seemed to me to be like sparks of light when I heard you read it."

"Yes, it is not an easy thing for me lately. Too many burdens."

She noticed her father felt it also and he nodded his head. The council's attacks on the young preachers, and the magistrate's personal attacks on her due to the incident from the past. So many burdens lately.

She prayed in her heart, *Lord, help us.*

❧

Remy slowed his pace. The pain was more severe today, sharper than he had experienced before. *Why had he come to Zurich, anyway?* He kept asking himself that question. *Was it a mistake? And now the question of his father.* Hans kept insisting that Remy go to see him. Remy mumbled to himself as he limped along. He could hear his brother's voice insisting, "Go see our father, he asks for you."

He wasn't ready. He knew exactly how his father would react; he was predictable that way. *Or was he?*

What Remy heard in his mind was "be strong and continue," so he did. He headed for his spot in the woods outside the city walls, hoping to see the monk. It surprised him that he enjoyed the company of the man and that they had things in common. "We are both homeless," he said aloud. "I guess that makes us companions, in a strange way."

He found the spot in the woods they called home and lay down on the cold ground hoping for relief from the pain.

There was some but not what he'd hoped for. He reflected on a time when he was young, about thirteen. His father had challenged him to prove that he could survive in the wild. The challenge was to make a shelter, start a fire, find game, cook it, stay overnight, and return to the city. Remy found satisfaction in this memory. He knew it had pleased his father when he completed the challenge. His father was proud that day.

But Remy's thoughts darkened when he considered the barriers that had sprung up between them. They hadn't spoken in years. The barriers hadn't been discussed, and they had grown bigger and wider in Remy's mind. He had a broken heart, and he didn't know what to do with it. Maybe he should go back to his beginnings, back to his father's home. Maybe that's where he would finish. He was falling asleep when he heard the words again: "be strong and continue." This time, he recognized it as his father's voice.

In his sleep, Remy entered a domain somewhere between dreams and sleep. He floated between two worlds, committed to neither. His father's face appeared, speaking words said long ago: "Remy, you'll never amount to anything." He asked of the face, "Is it true? Am I that person that you speak of?" And he felt as if a dagger had pierced his soul. He awoke for a bit, then fell again into a near sleep. Then he saw his father say, "I'm proud of you, son," and Remy remembered the times he had said that. Next, Hans's voice came up: "Go to your father." And now he heard, "Go back," and he knew he must. He fell into a welcome sleep.

Chapter 8

Cause us to stand to our own conscience clear
cause us to be the thing we appear

"Priscilla," Jakob called out as he walked through the front door.

Priscilla hurried out of the herb-drying room, brushing bits of herbs from her skirt, carrying the fragrance of them with her as she moved into the kitchen. "Did you deliver the priest's tapestry?"

"Two of the apprentices and I took it to him after borrowing the neighbor's cart."

"Was he happy with it? Did it look like it belonged where it was placed?"

"Yes, He was very pleased. He gushed over it. You know how he starts speaking in that animated way?" Priscilla nodded, listening. "I told him that you were involved in the design and workmanship. He looked surprised. Then he said, 'A woman's work.' He looked at it again and he gushed more. After that, here's what he said, 'Your daughter would make a very good Catholic.'"

Priscilla put her hands on her hips. "Oh Papa, did he really say that? Are you playing a joke?" She smiled at him, waiting for him to confess that he was joking. When he didn't, she said with a little laugh, "Well, I have never been a Catholic, and I never will be."

Jakob continued, "He says that about me nearly every time we are together. He will say, 'Jakob,' in a very serious way. But of course, I know the joke is coming, so I wait for it. 'Jakob, you should become a Catholic.' I shake my head and he laughs. It's our ritual, I suppose." Her father chuckled.

Later that evening, Priscilla sat mending clothing to help one of the new peasant families.

Her father looked up from the book he was reading and announced, "I am calling a meeting of the larger community of the brethren. It is well-needed. As I walk around the city, those of our community stop me with questions. They have heard stories about Felix and Conrad's problems with the council. Many tales are circulating, most of them half-truths. We will meet Thursday at the guild hall. I expect it will be a good-sized group. None of our homes will be adequate."

The word passed from house to house. That Thursday the brethren came, filling up the hall until there was only room to stand. Priscilla scanned the room, happy to see many new faces, including many women who often stayed away due to their responsibilities at home. They let their husbands attend and got reports of what had transpired. But the meeting tonight was an important one and almost everyone came out.

From behind Priscilla came Katrina's voice: "You look happy," she said.

Priscilla greeted Katrina and her husband with, "I am pleased to see you. You appear to be in fine health these days, friend. Join me." She made room for them. Barbara soon arrived and the women chatted about their day.

"Priscilla, remember when we used to put your poems to music and sing them a cappella?" Barbara asked. "I miss that time. Have you written any new ones lately?"

Katrina added, "I miss them also. Are you not writing anymore?"

"No, the writing has dropped off," Priscilla answered. "I have many other duties; I just don't seem to have the time." She knew these were excuses, but she also knew she didn't have it in her to write now, and she mourned the loss.

The meeting started with the usual freedom for all to offer a song or a scripture, so Barbara stood and led a song everyone knew. She sang out in her beautiful lilting voice and the others joined in. Some took parts and added to the wonder of an old song remembered.

When the song ended, Barbara leaned toward Priscilla, "If only we had some poetry." She winked.

One more song was sung, then Jakob stepped forward from where he was seated in the crowd. "There have been many stories floating about. Tonight, we will put an end to many of them and give a picture of what has been happening between our brothers and the city governors. We will hear from Conrad and Felix now."

Conrad was the first to speak. "It feels good to gather tonight among friends and brethren, to share our lives and our story. I see some who are new to us, and I welcome you. Here we can freely speak of our minds and hearts, but that is not the case in the city square. Friends, I know many have heard of the opposition from the members of the city council who have let it be known that they stand against our message. Not all the council, but some. They are not in agreement with what we preach in the market and the public square. They stand against not only our beliefs, but our freedom to express them publicly. But Felix and I agree . . ." Conrad stopped a moment for emphasis. "That we will not turn back from the gospel and the scripture that is clear on baptism. It is not for babies. It is only for those who have believed. We will live by the bible."

Many looking on, most of them peasants, cheerfully agreed. Conrad continued, "Because of our efforts, we have seen lives changed, people transformed because they heard and acted upon the gospel we preach. This very day, as I ended the preaching in the square, a woman approached me. Her story was heartwarming and affirming of our shared mission. She spoke of how she and her husband had been at odds for years. He was lost in drink and would beat her and their children mercilessly. She pointed to the Gross Muenster and said she had been a member of the old church, yet she never felt her heart was changed by its doctrine. She said she had tried her best to be a good person, but confessed she made no progress in getting along with her husband or being a good wife to him. One day, she heard us preaching. From that time on, as she walked through the square, she would listen to us and others speaking about God. She said she hadn't heard anyone speak about faith with authority and yet with love. The message of knowing God drew her." Here he spoke with emotion in his voice: "This woman began to cry as she spoke of the changes that had happened in her. She began to believe in a personal Christ as she listened to the word of God spoken in the square. As she came to know Christ, her heart was changed, and her attitude toward her husband and children softened. The stony heart within became a heart of flesh, as she said, and she began to love her husband once again."

Heads nodded all around the room. Conrad continued, "Her husband noticed the changes, and because of her faith in the Lord and her prayers, he came to believe also. She and her husband are here tonight, yes? Would you please stand and be acknowledged by those in attendance?" They stood, and humbly bowed their heads, receiving the group's appreciation. "This is only one of many stories we hear. Lives are being transformed by faith in Christ. It's all because we stand in the public square and preach the good news, despite those who disagree." Conrad nodded toward Felix.

The crowd erupted with excitement as Felix walked to the front of the room to take his turn. "It's true! That which we preach has changed lives. But our lives have changed also. We now have a fire within us, one that consumes us. We speak of healing and the source of healing. We speak to the pain of those listening, to the peasants and their struggles." With this, he nodded to some of the peasants in attendance. Their response was noisy again.

One of the peasants called out, "You have a voice that should be heard!"

Felix nodded to him and went on, "We want to see a change in our city. For many long years, it has been the norm that the church and the government were one. It was a marriage of the two. If you were a citizen of the canton of Zurich, you were obligated to baptize your baby. It was and still is the law. If you are baptized, you are then a Christian. We say no to this. We want the freedom to choose when we are baptized. This is a great undertaking, of course, but with God all things are possible. Is this not true, brothers and sisters?" Again, the crowd called out their agreement.

Felix continued, "The Swiss have always been a strong and independent people. We won our independence from the Holy Roman Empire because we are a valiant people. We stood for our right to be a separate people and we won that right. Did we not?"

There were nods all around and a shout or two from the peasants and the others.

"And this is our only desire, freedom. Freedom to worship as our consciences call us to, freedom to believe, live, and speak to others about our beliefs. This is our cry today, and every day. Freedom!" Cheers broke out again.

Finally, Jakob stood to quiet the crowd. Then a song rang out, free and clear. Priscilla was caught up in the excitement of the evening, watching the faces around her and listening to the comments that flowed around her. Then she happened to look at her father and saw that he wasn't joining in the merriment. She decided to ask him about it later.

After the meeting ended, people from the community lingered at the guild, commenting about and reveling in all that had happened that night. As Priscilla watched, she began to brood over her father's reaction. Later, when all had gone, they locked the guild hall and started the walk home. Jakob then spoke about what was on his mind.

"I know I have said this before: the young men don't know our history."

She held her breath. *Did he mean those who had gone before, the martyrs? Was that what he meant?* At home and settled in, she asked him more.

"It was an exciting night, and all were deeply inspired, but you didn't join in. Tell me why, Father?" She braced for the answer.

"They don't know how those who have gone before us have suffered."

"Do you mean the martyrs?"

"Yes, those who have died for their beliefs. We have read their stories, haven't we? I'm thinking of Jan Hus and Jerome of Prague in the last century; both burned at the stake. And earlier in the twelfth century, the Waldenses who started as street preachers like our friends, Felix and Conrad. Many died, considered heretics."

"In the past, it would have been the Catholics in charge. They would have been responsible for those martyred. Wouldn't they?"

"True, Priscilla. They were in control at the time. I believe those who have power now are capable of the same tyranny. It's in the heart of man. We must all fight that which is in our heart." He looked at her with weary eyes. "Our trust must be in the Lord for the outcome."

Later that night, she lay in bed, unable to sleep. She thought about the meeting and what her father had said. In the past, the Brotherhood had lived in peace, but now perhaps they would be called to suffer. *Before Felix and Conrad, our group was just an ember of fire, but those two have changed things. The young men burn with passion. Where might this take us?* She shuddered at her imaginings. *What would the future hold?*

With all the tension, she was unable to sleep. She tossed and turned and fretted about the future. Finally, lying there with her eyes open, she decided to look at her poetry. She threw off the covers and got out of bed, shivering at the cold of the room. Wrapping a blanket about her arms, she walked quietly, not wanting to wake her father in the next room. He slept lightly some nights. She tiptoed to her little desk and lit a candle. With the flickering light illuminating the room, she sat at the desk and searched for a poem written in better times. She was still somewhere between sleep and a place of not being entirely awake when she found it. There it was, the partially finished poem, all but forgotten because of where her life had taken her.

Reading over the piece slowly, she lingered, meditating on it. Then she read it out loud to herself quietly: "What room is there for troubled fear? I know my Lord and he is near; and he will light my candle." *A good start*, she thought. The other phrase she had was "Fret not thyself." *How should they fit together?* She mused over that problem for a while as it lay before her on the desk. *That first part speaks*, she thought. But she didn't seem able to complete the work. She set her pen down in frustration and rested her chin on her fist.

She felt she didn't have what it took to write these days, and she wasn't sure she would ever regain it. She decided to read it over once more, even more slowly. No, it wasn't there, the spark she needed to make it come alive. Maybe she was too close to her fear these days. It was no longer in the future. It was here, at their doorstep. She thought about the other line, "Fret not Thyself . . ." *Was God speaking this to her? Yes, He must be, and she needed to listen.* "Fret not Thyself . . ." She was hearing it now. Easy enough to write it on a piece of paper; practicing it was the difficult part.

❧

Chapter 9

She woke slowly, remembering how she had worried deep into the night, brooding over different scenarios. *What if this happens, what if that?* She had troubled herself for hours before coming to a place of peace. But now questions came to her mind again. *What about the young men?* A bit of anger returned, and she fretted more. Finally, she chased away the thoughts gnawing at her. She determined not to allow herself to go there again. There were too many questions about the future.

She got up and went to the window, seeing that the morning had opened the sky and the sun was beginning to show its face through the mist on the mountains. That brought her more peace. She lingered for a moment, enjoying and reflecting on the image. Then reality set in, and her responsibilities at the guild called her. She hurried to get out of the house and started for the guild.

Due to the tensions in the city, the work of the guild had slowed, but now Priscilla and her father were back at it, trying to catch up. "Father, where are Jonas and Mattias today?" Priscilla asked as she took her place at the loom.

"This is why I have needed you here. I received word that they were leaving this morning to fight."

"Peasant wars, again," she said, disappointment in her voice.

Jakob sighed. "I am not happy with it, but the peasants have their convictions also. I just wish it didn't involve going to war."

Priscilla agreed. She began working at the weaving that must be finished and go out that very day. She knew her father needed her badly now, but she wished he had called her to work on a piece of tapestry. The weaving could be mundane; tapestry was what she enjoyed. Her home, her garden, and this work were her delights. She was deep in her thoughts when she realized she had made a mistake in the weaving. Realizing she was too removed from her work, she chided herself. She needed to concentrate and put her thoughts on the shelf. That's what they told the apprentices. She needed to follow her own advice.

As she worked to remedy her mistake, she saw one of the councilmen walk into the guild. He passed by her work area and nodded in acknowledgment. She paused, wondering why William was at the guild. Perhaps it was official business. She hadn't seen him lately; their lives rarely intersected. When his son was an apprentice at the guild, she saw him more. She didn't think about it again until later at dinner.

"Did you see William at the guild today?" Jakob said, pulling up his chair to the large table.

"I did. News of his son? How is he fairing?"

"No, he wanted to comment on the council and their treatment of our young men. He said he was sorry for the events of late and how they must make us suffer. He said he speaks up for us, and he wants to know that not everyone agrees with the council's treatment."

"That's kind of him. I have always thought of him as a good man. We'll see if that makes a difference." She had her doubts, but caught herself, thinking of the prayer from the night before when she asked the Lord to change her heart.

"I have an idea! We should find a barn to hide in. We could burrow down in the hay to stay warm," Jorg told Remy as they settled into their little home under the tree. "It's getting colder out here."

"What if the landlord finds us and he carries a pitchfork?" Remy asked apathetically.

Jorg responded with his enormous laugh. "We would have to take steps to avoid that!"

Remy studied his friend with questions in his mind. Jorg seemed different lately, not as low and burdened as he had before. Remy looked at Jorg and puzzled over this.

Jorg spoke up. "Do you hope to marry someday, Remy?"

Remy stared at Jorg, even more puzzled.

"I want to marry!" Jorg spoke it as if it were a proclamation.

"Marry . . . monks do not marry."

"Oh, you think because I have worn the robes of a monk, I don't think of such things, of love and romance?" Remy looked on with curiosity. Jorg continued, "I had a love once." He glanced at Remy. "Ha, I see you don't believe the monk. Do you think I lie? I will tell you about her. You will have to believe me, yes?"

"Take it easy, monk. Tell me your story. I need a good story about now." Remy fidgeted in his resting place, trying to find a comfortable spot that might ease his ongoing pain. "Go on," he said impatiently.

"She was beautiful. Her name was Elizabeth. She lived near my father's property. Sometimes we would walk in the woods near my home, and I would hold her hand as we walked."

"Oh, here comes the romance part."

"I loved her from the moment I laid eyes on her. Did I say she was beautiful?"

"Yes, yes that's what you said. This story isn't going anywhere now. Does it have a good end?"

"No. Her father didn't want me as a husband for his daughter. He said I was too boisterous, too loud."

"Who, you?" Remy said, laughing.

"And my father wanted me to be a monk. It was his dream to have a son as a monk. But it wasn't mine." He said the last part in an uncharacteristically quiet way. "The last time I saw Elizabeth, I told her I loved her, and she looked up at me with those big brown eyes of hers and whispered that she felt the same."

"I see it now . . . those big brown eyes looking up at you," Remy said with sarcasm, meaning it as a joke.

But the big monk didn't take it that way. Looking at Remy in a menacing way, he said "Do you mock me?"

Not wanting to anger a man of Jorg's size, Remy hurriedly said, "What happened to her?"

"I don't know. Shortly afterward I was taken to the monastery, and it became my life." Jorg sighed and looked off into the distance.

"Yes, fathers have dreams, don't they?" Remy added bitterly.

Nothing was said for a while. Then Jorg said what was foremost in his heart: "I am looking for my people."

"What do you mean?" Remy asked.

The question went unanswered.

Chapter 10

The mountains hold their breath

Changes had come to the Brotherhood: new faces, new intensity, and stories of lives changed. The crowds continued to gather around Felix and Conrad as they read the broadsides and preached in the square. It was colder now, fall was upon them, but the people still came, eager to hear what was shared. The young men saw they were taking it into their hearts. Barbara and Priscilla often joined the crowds, wanting to hear what was being preached.

One day, when Felix was done speaking, they approached him. Priscilla gathered her cloak around her shoulders against the wind that had come up. "Felix, good day," she said. "We see the crowd is very large today."

"Yes, this is our experience more and more, the crowds are growing, despite the weather," Felix said excitedly.

"What did you read? I didn't recognize it," Barbara asked.

"It's a new broadside I finished printing just today. The people seemed to really receive it. We read both scripture and the broadsides to them. As you know, most do not have the ability to read the scripture, because it's in Latin. We are happy to give them God's word and they seem happy to hear it, especially today. Then they can decide for themselves if they will believe. We don't compel one way or another. We leave it to the Holy Spirit. We only pray that the Spirit will grip their hearts as He has gripped ours."

With that, he looked up to see snow falling in large billowy flakes. He watched as it slowly fell to the ground. "Ah, the first snow, and I believe it's promising more," he said.

"Blessings to you, brother," Priscilla responded. "Barbara and I must hurry on now and attend to our homes. We will see you at the next guild meeting. I believe it's tomorrow." Priscilla and Barbara waved and hastened on.

The bigger crowds brought a variety of ideas and viewpoints. Peasants with heavy hearts were joining the brethren at their gatherings. Expectations for change from the peasant wars had not been met and now they suffered lack. Some hadn't given up on taking up arms to fight for what they thought should come to them, their rights to their land and the freedom to work it. So in addition to the tension in the city, there were conflicts and differences of opinion within the Brotherhood. Into this simmering pot now came someone who was to bring more change.

The meeting started late that night, and the guild hall was at capacity. The man arrived silently, walked to the front of the room, and sat with intensity. All eyes were on him. A deep silence, tinged with fear, enveloped the room. People around the room put their heads together and whispered, "Who is he?"

Priscilla asked the same question: *Who was this commanding man, dressed in the robes of a monk?*

Although the meeting had started, nothing flowed. The man's presence hung over them with unspoken words. When it was obvious that something must be said, Jakob walked to the front of the room. "Is there something that you want to say, brother?" he asked.

The man stood and said in a way that commanded, and yet was said with a whisper of prayer in it, "I want to know . . ." He stopped and looked around at the people. The crowd held its breath. "I want to know, am I amongst the people of God?"

The crowd exhaled.

After the meeting, Priscilla watched her father, Conrad, and the monk talk as they sat in the ornate chairs that had been a part of the guild hall for untold years. The chairs had been handed down for generations, as had their faith been handed down from generation to generation. There they sat, her father representing the Old Brotherhood; a monk from the church which had in the past caused problems for their group; and young Conrad, from whom they hoped would come a new beginning for the Brotherhood.

She tried to listen as the monk related his story. She was close enough to hear Conrad say, "Where do you stay, brother?"

"Call me Jorg. I am no longer connected to the monastery."

"We call each other brother here. Where have you stayed since leaving the monastery?"

"I have been sleeping under God's creation, in the woods outside the city."

"We will remedy that. You will stay with my wife and me. We have room in our home. It is this group's way to offer a place to those in need. It's too cold to sleep outside."

"There's just one thing." Jorg looked hopefully at Conrad. "I have been sharing my spot in the woods with another who needs shelter. Would there be room for him?"

Later that evening, after a small meal of cold fowl, Jakob and Priscilla talked over the day's events. "Daughter, this evening was one of the most remarkable of nights. When the monk walked in none of us knew what to expect, did we?" Jakob paused to recall the scene. "I have spent many days in that old hall, but tonight will be one to stand out among the many. Let me tell you what I felt. I must think of the right words. It seemed to me as if the ancient walls of that old room stopped to listen, to record that moment." He stopped to shake his head. "It was as if there was a shift and something new was emerging, something that cannot be stopped."

Priscilla studied her father's face and saw awe there.

"The young men are leading us to a new place, just as we thought. It's time to join the saints that have come before us."

Jorg and Remy settled into Conrad and Barbara's attic room. "Luxury compared to our former accommodations,"

Remy said as he glanced around before quickly hopping into the bed provided for him.

"Beds, that's something we haven't experienced for too long, huh, Remy?" Jorg said, making an unsuccessful attempt to speak quietly. "These beds are better than the ones at the monastery. Those were hard. It was part of our disciplines, you know." Settling into the bed, Jorg pulled the covers up to his chin, adding, "These are nice and soft. What do you think, Remy?"

The only response was a loud snore.

Chapter 11

It slipped like sunshine through
my eager hands

Barbara served Conrad and Jorg hefty pieces of freshly baked bread and poured them large mugs of goat milk. They each took a few bites. But anxious to converse, Conrad asked Jorg, "Tell me your story. How did you come to join our meeting?"

Jorg said, "I am from the House of Jakob. My father was very well-off and a great lover of the Roman church. He had always wanted a son who would be a priest. So he sent me to Chur and the monastery of Saint Lucian. I had mixed feelings. I, too, loved the church, but I wasn't sure of my vocation. The prayer and the liturgy were very beautiful. They fed my soul. But after five or six years I began to hear of the corruption in Rome. And I became aware of monks I knew who broke their vows. They had women in the village and were given to drink. I felt confused. Doubts surfaced. I struggled for years with dark thoughts and terrible temptations myself. I was miserable. My only hope was prayer. But as I prayed, questions haunted me."

Jorg stopped as Remy came down the stairs, barely awake, crashing into their conversation. "Oh sorry, I overslept," he said.

"Sit, Remy. Barbara will bring you breakfast," Conrad said.

Barbara came with the food and Conrad and Jorg watched as Remy devoured it, like a man who hadn't eaten regularly for months. They saw him wipe his mouth with his sleeve, then look up, embarrassed. He seemed relieved to see Barbara had gone into the other room, unaware of his lack of social grace. Minutes later, when Barbara returned to pick up his dishes, Remy had reclaimed his manners, thanking her profusely with his usual charm.

She laughed at the lavish outpouring of gratitude.

Conrad said, "Remy, did you sleep well?"

"Better than could be imagined. You have a very peaceful home."

Conrad turned back to Jorg. "What do you need? What can I do for you?"

"You speak of the scripture . . . of the bible when you preach," Jorg said. "It looks to me it is key to your understanding. I know very little of the things you speak of. I have a great need to understand the bible. Will you teach me?"

"Did you not receive instruction in the scripture in the monastery?"

"We received very little. And I don't read well. I confess I am very ignorant about the scripture."

"We will start tomorrow."

The next day Conrad opened his bible to Genesis and Jorg fired off questions. Remy joined them. He listened but pretended not to.

At one point Barbara hurried through the room. Conrad said, "Barbara, you need to sit down and rest. Do your legs still ache?" She nodded. "Then when we go to preach, we will talk to Priscilla. She needs to attend to you with her herbs."

The following day Priscilla walked along the streets, now lined with the stark and barren trees of fall. No matter. She thought the mountains were always beautiful and chose to focus on them. At Conrad and Barbara's, she sat with Barbara. Time was taken to share about their homes and what food was to their liking lately, with Priscilla praising Greta's cooking skills.

Eventually, Barbara began to describe her symptoms, including swollen ankles and pain in her legs. Priscilla said, "I know just the remedies for that condition, I've treated it often. I've brought nettles I have prepared. Add water to make a paste, apply it to your legs and cover them. Do this daily for five days. I think that will be adequate. This is associated with your drawing close to delivering your child. Do you look forward to being a mother?"

"I do. I am more excited by the day."

"I remember being a young mother, although it seems so very long ago," Priscilla mused.

"What happened to your children, Priscilla?"

"I lost them to the plague . . . and my husband also."

Barbara took Priscilla's hand, sharing her sorrows. Then she remembered: "Oh, I meant to tell you, when we took the monk to live with us, he told us of his friend who badly needed a place also. They were living in the woods."

"Living in the woods? This time of year?" Priscilla said.

"Yes. He has come to live with us as well. We were glad to offer shelter. That's been our way, hasn't it, sister, to help those in our group who have fallen on hard times. But now we are welcoming those from the outside. It feels good to care for others."

Priscilla nodded in agreement and Barbara continued, "This man that Jorg brought with him was in the peasant wars. He has a wound on his upper leg. It's bad, Priscilla. It looks infected to me. He was very reluctant, but I insisted he see you. He walks the city with that leg, limping badly. I think it is worse than it was a few days ago."

Just then, Remy came limping in. "Remy, please join us. This is the woman I mentioned who treats with herbs. Let her look at your leg." Barbara stood and offered him her chair. "Sit just here."

Examining him, Priscilla looked at Remy with eyes that saw beyond the outer man. She saw a man with scars on his face, but she wondered at the inner scars she saw in his eyes. Looking in her kit, she was pleased to see she had the needed herbs to make a poultice to pull out the infection. She carefully prepared it, then gently applied the dressing. Remy winced at being touched. Priscilla supposed that, besides the pain, he had not been touched in a caring way for a long time.

"This is really bad, young man," Priscilla observed. "If allowed to go on much longer the outcome could have been dire. Perhaps you would have lost your leg."

Remy cringed at the possibility. "That cannot happen to me! I'm a soldier!"

"Was this wound from the wars of the peasants?" Priscilla asked.

Looking down, Remy didn't answer.

"What did you do before the war?"

"I was a cobbler. That's how I was trained."

"My father would like to meet you," Priscilla said, looking at Barbara. "Remember I told you, Barbara? He has been looking for a cobbler. He intends to help the peasants by providing shoes."

She said to Remy, "I know you have a special interest in the peasants, knowing their plight and their poverty. They need shoes badly. Why don't you come tonight to the meeting and there you can talk to Jakob, my father. I will introduce you. I hope you will come."

Later, while they walked through the city, Jorg turned to Remy. "I am going to the meeting tonight. Will you come along?"

"No, you go. I'm not religious like you. You will be more comfortable there."

"Oh, come on. What will it hurt?" Jorg answered.

"Will there be women there?"

"Maybe wives for us, huh?" Jorg said mischievously, poking Remy in the ribs.

"I didn't say wives, I said women."

Jorg shook his head. "I don't think you will meet those kinds of women in this group."

Anna walked through the house looking for Fredrik. She found him in his library, absorbed as he often was in a book. She approached the desk with trepidation. Lately he seemed especially volatile. She was never sure what mood he would be in. She thought going to the meeting tonight without an explanation wasn't the best idea given his current unpredictability. She had to tell him about Priscilla.

"I'm going to spend a little time with Priscilla tonight."

"Who?"

"Priscilla. I told you about her. I met her at the market, and we have become friends."

"Oh, yes. You mentioned her," he said, without looking up.

"I'm going now, my housework is done for the night."

He said nothing, just nodded. She started for the door, but he surprised her. "Just a moment." She turned and watched him get up and approach her. What did he want? She hoped he hadn't changed his mind. She was looking forward to the meeting.

Fredrik drew close to her, softly stroked her arm. "Don't stay too long," he said. "I was hoping to spend time together tonight." He looked deeply into her eyes, and she marveled at how soon he could change and become the charming Fredrik. Tonight, she was conflicted. On one hand, he always caused her to melt when he was like this toward her. But a part of her still felt shame and guilt about her life with Fredrik. "I'll be back soon," she said softly and turned to go.

"I will be waiting for you," he said, watching her leave.

Leaning up against a wall, Remy watched as Anna walked into the room, sat down, and looked out a window. He remembered her. She was the young woman who saved the kitten. That day, he hadn't noticed how beautiful she was. Now he watched the flickering candle highlight her features. She was delicate, and yet she was strong. With that thought, he was drawn to her even more. She liked to rescue homeless things. That would be him. He decided to talk to her. He had approached many women, usually with bravado, but tonight he felt uncharacteristically shy and awkward. Walking over to Anna, he blurted out, "I saw you with the kitten." She swirled around with an alarmed look on her face.

"Who are you?"

Attempting to redeem himself, Remy gave her a charming smile that lit up his face, "I'm Remy."

Anna didn't see the charm. She only wanted her secret kept. She retorted, "It's none of your business." She turned once more toward the window. Remy, taken aback, nodded and moved back to the wall. Anna glanced at him for a moment and he looked away. Feeling uncomfortable, Remy gave his attention to a nearby conversation but kept his eyes on Anna.

Then Jorg walked into the room. Remy saw Anna stare at Jorg with a puzzled look. He wondered why she had an interest in him. Not one to give up, he walked over to Jorg, thinking maybe he could get her attention that way. She looked at him dismissively and turned her head away again.

"Jorg, do you know who that woman is?"

"I don't know her name, but I saw her in the crowd when I went with Conrad when he preached in the square."

"She's a beauty," Remy said, his eyes trained on her again.

"I told you there would be wives for us here," Jorg said, his lips curling into a smile. Remy continued to look at Anna from time to time, making plans. Someday, he'd take her in his arms.

Later that evening, before leaving, Anna asked Priscilla, "Who is that man?" gesturing toward Jorg.

"He's one of the men staying at Conrad's home."

"I saw him at the church praying. He wore the robes of a monk." Anna stared at him, then said, "Tonight he seems a different man." Her thoughts held her in a sort of suspension as she looked at him.

Anna walked to the rectory thinking about the monk and how surprised she was to see him at the meeting. He looked different from the tortured man she'd seen in the church. There was a peace about him now. Then she realized with alarm that it was very late; she needed to hurry. Fredrik would be wondering about her. He probably was angry.

Quietly opening the door, she tried to slip into the dark house undetected. She took off her shoes and tiptoed across the room toward the stairs. But in the low light she saw Fredrik sitting in the dark and he greeted her with, "What took you so long? I've been sitting here watching for you." He stood and blocked her way. She could smell drink on his breath. She decided she wouldn't let anything bother her tonight. It had been a wonderful night to remember, seeing the monk and his change. "I would like to go to bed, I'm tired," she said looking up at him.

"What do you do at this Priscilla's home so late in the evening?" His voice sounded threatening.

"We talk." She was always vague about her visits to Priscilla.

"About what?"

"Many things."

"Is she your age?"

"No, she could be my mother's age."

Frederik looked at her suspiciously. Hoping to control the situation, she said, "Tonight they had music."

"Music! Who are these people?"

She realized her mistake.

He said it again, "Music?"

She thought he seemed jealous.

Then he said, "I don't think you need to see this Priscilla again." Turning his back to her, he added, "I'll be waiting for you upstairs. You will come to my bed tonight. I have waited long enough."

❧

Chapter 12

For the comfort of forgiveness

Priscilla inspected her new stores of herbs. Some she had gathered from her garden behind her home. Others she had found in the woods and the hills outside the city walls. She hoped she had enough for those who would need healing that winter.

In her mind, she listed the usual needs and the remedies: yarrow, rosemary, and sweet violet for Remy's wound and the wounds of others as the peasant wars continued. Peony, pennyroyal, and larkspur for fevers. She had a good amount for the coming season that would soon be upon them. Wild thyme, basil, dill, and mandrake for headaches. On that list, she noted the names of those who often needed them, with Bella, her next-door neighbor being one.

As she thought of each herb, the flowers they represented were vivid in her thoughts, as was her delight in caring for them. As she moved to the other room, their fragrance followed her like faithful pets. The ones she would need today she prepared to process in her mortar and pestle, grinding them to the necessary degree.

Afterward, she visited Barbara to check on her two patients. Barbara greeted her at the door. Priscilla said, "I see you are feeling better. Are you up and about most of the day?"

"I am back to my old routine most of the time. I still must rest more. A nap is needed, though I resist it."

"I recommend you take that time to rest. Let's check your ankles. Why don't you sit there?" Barbara got situated and Priscilla knelt to examine her legs. "There is still some swelling in the ankles, but your color is good, and I think you're on the mend. May I ask about Remy? How does he seem?"

"He is better, still limping a bit. He is doing some work for Conrad on the outside of the house in the back. He'll be in soon to eat. I've been thinking it would be good for him to set down roots. He should find a wife, don't you think?"

But before Priscilla could answer, Barbara decided to take the conversation in a different direction, and she said, "Priscilla, you don't do midwifery anymore? I can't talk you into it. I will need someone soon, you know."

"There are others in the community that are just as good or probably better than I was," Priscilla answered, taking a seat.

Barbara leaned forward. "I don't believe that, sister. Your herbal knowledge is superior to all others." Barbara cast a quizzical look at Priscilla. "Is there something you want to share about this? I don't know why you would walk away from midwifery when in the past, you have said . . ."

Priscilla cut her off. "It's not something I want to discuss."

Surprised by her friend's abrupt response, Barbara sat back for a moment, then continued, "Yes, of course. I just want you to know if you need to talk, I'm a good listener. You are a dear friend, Priscilla, and always in my prayers. Let me call Remy in."

Remy entered the room and Priscilla, glad for the reprieve from Barbara's questions, observed that he did indeed still limp but had improved. "How does the leg feel, Remy?" she asked kindly.

"Much better, ma'am," he said, taking his hat off and holding it in his hand. "I am grateful for your care."

"You will need to continue to apply the herbs I provided for the rest of the week. Then I believe you may stop, and I will check in with you early next week."

"Thank you again."

Priscilla smiled. "I understand you had a conversation with my father about the cobbler work. I have seen some of your fine work."

"Well, the shoes made for the peasants will be simpler than those, ma'am," he said humbly. "I am happy to be of service as I am a peasant myself. I served in the battles to fight for change for our people but that hasn't been as successful as we hoped," he said, turning his head away.

Priscilla, not knowing what to say, excused herself and started for the door. Barbara stopped her to say goodbye and to remind her that she was available for more conversation about midwifery if she liked.

Snow began to fall, and the cobblestones were wet and slippery as Priscilla started up the hill. She struggled to keep her balance. This slowed her down, giving her time to think. She considered what a good and faithful friend Barbara had been. Priscilla's secret weighed heavily today and, as she walked on, she relived the experience of meeting the magistrate on this very street. Her thoughts made her shudder. It came to her that her burden would be lighter if she shared it with her trusted friend. She decided to turn around and started back toward her friend's home.

Hurrying along, Priscilla felt it was time to get her secret out in the open. Yet as she walked on, she felt a sense of dread at having to confess her failure. She paused before the door but then knocked.

Opening the door, Barbara was surprised to see her. "Please come in. Let's talk."

Sitting facing Barbara, Priscilla got right to it. "Barbara, I think you are a friend I can trust." She looked deeply into Barbara's eyes and breathed a sigh of relief. "I need a friend who will stick closer than a brother right now. Would that be you?"

Barbara nodded. "Of course."

"I set something in motion that we are all suffering from."

"How so?"

"It's my fault we're being treated so harshly by the magistrate. He will do anything to bring revenge on me and the others."

"We will not think about that now. Tell me what happened the night Sarah died," Barbara said.

"Rumors have circulated even among our community members. Have you heard them?"

"I don't give much attention to gossip," Barbara said with concern.

Priscilla looked at her as if to gauge if Barbara was still with her. If she knew the full story would she side with the gossips? Priscilla decided she must get it out in the open.

She began, "I wasn't feeling well, and I tried to beg off and hand the birth to someone I knew. The magistrate's wife, Sarah, wouldn't hear of it. She said I was the best and wanted my services, so I agreed. Did you know her?"

"I would see her around the city at times, but I never spoke with her," Barbara responded.

"I had attended another birth of hers. She struggled that time and delivered after a long labor. This labor started out routinely and for that I was relieved."

Barbara nodded.

"But as the hours went on, I could see she wasn't progressing, and I began to be concerned. It was into the second night and well over twenty-four hours into the labor. Bruno made the situation even more intense, pacing outside the door. Ordinarily, husbands go about their business and let the midwife have her way, bowing to her expertise. That wasn't the case with this birth. He wanted to come into the room, and I told him it wasn't appropriate. He cursed at me but then became quiet. A deep exhaustion came over me,

I suppose the result of my not being completely recovered from the sickness I had known. She still wasn't progressing so I decided to try a herb I don't usually use, one that had been suggested to me. But in my weakened state, I believe I took up the wrong herb. It acted quickly, and she grew weaker and weaker. I knelt by the bed, and I whispered to her, 'Trust in Jesus, dear woman. He will be your rescuer.' She replied, 'I have my faith and that's enough for me.'"

I watched her struggle, sinking deeper and deeper into that valley from which I knew she would never return. At the end, she cried out. With that, the magistrate rushed into the room. He looked at me and then at Sarah and said, "Is she . . . is she gone?"

He knew the answer by the look on my face. He fell upon his knees beside his wife, threw his arms around her, and laid his head on her breast. He gave a cry of anguish as I've never heard and wept over her. I have never seen a man with that level of emotional pain. Finally, he glared at me with an accusing look. I began to say weakly how sorry I was. He was furious. He cut me off and sent me away. I left his house in a state, fatigued with the ordeal. I stumbled home, sick with fatigue and sorrow. I returned to an empty house; my father had left for work. I staggered upstairs and went directly to bed to a fretful sleep. *What had I done?* I kept thinking. That's how it happened and why he hates me to this very day. And now, unfortunately, he has much power over us."

"I play it over and over in my head, Barbara. This has been such a weight. I wish I could go back and start again. Fix it, change the course of events, but that is not possible now." Priscilla looked down at her hands in her lap, then continued, "I don't like to show weakness. I've never been one to want to bare my soul to anyone. But with you, Barbara, I feel differently. I feel I can trust you. I haven't had anyone outside my father I could open up to. I've been foolish for not trusting you enough to share my burden, my sin."

"Priscilla you mustn't think of her death in that way. It was a mistake, pure and simple. A wrong choice made by someone in a weakened state."

Priscilla considered her friend's words. "Perhaps you are right. Perhaps I've made this into something it's not. I will have to think on it."

Barbara took Priscilla's hand, and said, "I want you to know I stand with you, and I support you. I am pleased you feel the freedom to share this with me. We should bear each other's burdens and I feel honored that you have shared yours with me."

Sitting beside Remy, Jorg said, "You are still at odds with your father?"

"Why do you ask?" Remy said perplexed.

"Last night you tossed and turned, keeping me awake."

Remy offered no apology.

"'Oh Hans, Hans, it's always Hans.' That's what you kept saying."

"My father is always bragging about Hans," Remy said.

"Who is this Hans?"

"My brother, the butcher. You've never met him?"

"No, how would I meet him?"

Remy shrugged his shoulders.

"I've had problems with *my* father," interjected Jorg, his face gloomy. "I haven't seen him for a long time. I figured after I left the monastery, he wouldn't care to see me."

Ignoring Jorg's comment, Remy said, "My father always compares me to my brother. I'm not Hans!" he said, agitated.

"You should meet with your father. It will make a difference."

Forgetting his earlier resolution, Remy said, "I think you have it wrong this time."

Jorg's suggestions stayed with Remy for the rest of the day. The next morning, feeling downhearted, he thought he should walk the city. But now, as if there were some line or force that drew him, he walked straight to the market and found himself in front of Hans's stall, watching him arranging the meat and other goods.

"Hans!" Remy said brusquely.

Hans turned around. "Remy, I didn't notice you there. There's something I wanted to tell you. Our father has been asking for you." Remy was taken aback. "You should go to see him. He's been talking about you all week."

"Maybe I don't want to see him."

Looking at his brother with impatience, Hans said, "Suit yourself, I'm just letting you know."

"You went to see Hans?" Jorg asked when Remy returned.

"How did you know?"

"I told you, I know things sometimes. What are you going to do?"

Remy was conflicted. His heart was cold and unfeeling; he felt something hard and dark within him.

*

Remy had almost forgotten the pain in his leg as he limped along. He would have to face his father—his disappointments in his son. He looked up to see the house in the distance, a modest peasant's home. Not at all like the more opulent homes like Conrad's he had been in recently. He was feeling both a sense of abhorrence about his plan and a feeling that things would be resolved, one way or another. Maybe he was in for a battle; maybe not. He reached the door. *Did he want to do this?*

Before he could answer that question, the door opened, and Hans stood before him saying, "So you've come."

"Yes, is he here?"

Remy watched his father approach the door and invite him in, his look surprised but guarded. They sat together for a time, neither speaking. Finally, his father said, "It's you, the deserter."

"I didn't desert. I thought you didn't want me to go in the first place." Remy wondered if his father wanted this time alone with him only to insult him.

His father spit out his next words: "You should have stayed here and worked as a cobbler. I told you it was a failed endeavor, the peasant wars. It was a waste. People have died, and for what?" They spent a few moments staring at each other. Then his father added, "I heard you are with the heretics."

"Who told you that?" Remy knew it was probably Hans. "They offered me a place and I took it." He wanted to say, *Which you didn't offer*, but thought better of it. "I was sleeping in the woods, and they have been kind."

"You should have stayed in Zurich. Now look at you, limping." To Remy's surprise, his father's gaze changed to one of compassion. "What are you doing about the wound? Somebody got you good, huh?"

"A local woman is treating me with herbs. She's good, the best in Zurich. She says it will heal but I must be patient."

"See to it that you follow her instructions. Come back next week, son. It will be good to see more of you. Will you stay in the city?"

"I have been asked to do some cobbling work." At that, something passed between them. There was a softening toward each other that they each longed for.

Chapter 13

I thought I had courage in the house
and patience to be quiet and endure

Barbara and Priscilla worked together in Barbara's kitchen to salt the meat to be shared that winter. Priscilla asked, "How does it go having the young men in your home? Do they disturb your peaceful routine?"

"They are quiet much of the time. Their personalities are so different. Remy is charming but he is also serious. And sometimes he is distant, seeming to mull over things that bother him. Jorg is the opposite. Everything about him is big: his voice, his height, his girth, and his heart. He is so focused on God. Conrad and the others feel entirely joined to him—a kindred spirit. It has been easy taking him in."

Barbara went on, "Jorg had questions about the guild. He knew that guilds were training places for the tradesmen, but he didn't know the connection of the guilds to faith. Conrad explained how for many years we had secretly met to discuss and practice our faith at the guilds and how some on the outside called us heretics because we met in homes to discuss the bible and spiritual writers from the past who are considered heretics by those outside our group.

"After that, Jorg said, in that gregarious way of his, 'If they say that about you, I join myself to you and your cause. I am also a heretic.' To which we all laughed. Conrad said we are not as they say; we are followers of Christ. Jorg's heart matches ours, Priscilla, so yes, we are enjoying him. As for Remy, we pray for him. He needs God's healing in his heart."

Thinking about healing and taking care to proceed with caution, Barbara said to Priscilla, "About your involvement in the meetings . . . it seems to me you have pulled back from things I always thought you excelled in, like teaching at the gatherings."

Barbara felt she could bring this up because of their recent shared trust. Though her friend had been reluctant to talk about this, she felt the need to challenge that reluctance. "In the past, we have all had a voice in the meetings. Haven't we agreed that the women's voices should be heard?" She paused. "Don't you have things in your heart that would be worthwhile to share?"

"I'm not certain I have that freedom," Priscilla answered.

"What is changed then?"

"We have had complaints by some of the men."

"What would your father say? He's our leader, under the headship of Jesus, of course. What does the Lord say? Wouldn't it be good for you to take it to prayer?"

It was a challenge. Priscilla felt it as she walked through the big wooden door of their home. She needed a few minutes to herself. Greta greeted her in her usual chatty way. Priscilla listened to be polite but wished to be alone. She excused herself and sat in her chair in the sitting room. She thought about what Barbara had said and began praying about it. *Was God using Barbara to speak to her again?* She needed to talk to her father. Jorg's abrupt entry into their lives had taken her to a greater place of questioning. Their past had been one of order and peace. Only months before they had had their meetings, their set ways, and their lives. Now all was turned upside down and there were many crowding into their lives looking for answers. There had been clashes, bickering, differences of opinions, and discord, and she had become confused by it all.

&

After the evening meal, she sensed her father seemed out of sorts. "Papa, how are you tonight? Problems at the guild?"

"Just the same problems I suppose," he answered. "The guild, the magistrate." As he said this, his countenance lightened, and he smiled at her.

She felt safe to bring up her problem.

"Father, do you still believe women should have a voice in the church? There has been criticism lately. I don't feel I have the freedom that I once had." She shared her struggles, the rumors, and the men that criticized her. When she finished, Jakob seemed heavy and burdened again.

"Why bring these things up, Priscilla? It doesn't seem to me to be a major issue right now, with all the pressure from the council and the things that are a burden at the hall."

Soon after, she went to bed carrying the sting of her father's words. She was troubled, but as she prayed, peace came with the words of a psalm that she had memorized. "On my bed, I remember you; I think of you through the watches of the night. Because you have been my help, I sing in the shadow of your wings. My soul clings to you." She held these words in her heart.

When he awoke, Jakob determined to speak with Priscilla about their conversation. He watched her fuss over breakfast. They both savored the luscious fragrance of the newly baked bread. Jakob watched as she cut two thick pieces, placed them on their plates, and added some cheese Greta had recently made. She put his dish before him. When she sat down he said, "Priscilla, I had a distressing night."

"How is that, Papa?" She looked at him with concern.

"I feel I've been unfair to you. I have not respected my daughter. You came to me with a worry and a rightful one. And I cast it aside."

She took a deep breath then let it out.

Jakob went on, "Priscilla, do you believe that you are called?"

"Of course, I am called. I have believed in Christ since I was a child, and I answered that call."

"No. I mean, do you feel that you have a call to teach in the meetings?"

"I don't know, much has happened over the years. I've been criticized by some of the men when I have spoken. Then came the incident with the birth and the magistrate's family," she said.

Jakob nodded compassionately. "I know that experience has been hard to endure."

"I suppose my sense of confidence has been undermined with all of it," she said.

Jakob regarded her with his kind eyes. "Why don't you take some time for prayer?" he suggested. "If God gives you something, you should share it at the next gathering. God has used you to speak and He will in the future. You have been given a gift."

❧

Conrad looked directly at Jorg. "It's your turn now," he said. Jorg stared at him with a puzzled expression, waiting. "You have watched me preach. Now it's time to tell your story to others."

"I don't feel confident in my reading skills, I don't think I could read a broadside to the people."

"It doesn't matter. Just tell your story. It's a powerful one, Jorg. Lives will be changed. Today we will go to the old church, and you will preach."

Later, standing in front of the Gross Muenster, Conrad said to Jorg, "This is where you will begin." He looked up at the big man. "I have taught you well and now you are on a new path. You will become the teacher."

Jorg swallowed hard, looked out at the crowd forming, then over at Conrad for reassurance. Conrad nodded, yet Jorg hesitated. The crowd was loud and raucous, and they were confused by the monk standing before them.

One of the peasants yelled out sarcastically, "What's your story, monk? Someone said you have joined these preachers here. What's that about? You left your comfortable life in the monastery? Sounds foolish to me." He laughed, as did his friends.

"I have peace now!" Jorg cried out, and the crowd heard his passion.

The peasant expected his friends to continue laughing, but they were looking at Jorg, anxious to hear his response.

Another man yelled, "You seem an honest man."

Jorg was encouraged by this. "Listen, friends!" he shouted out with his big voice. "Today I am here to announce something." He had their attention. "Maybe you don't know me, I am Jorg of the House of Jakob. I am announcing good news to all within the sound of my voice." Jorg was encouraged by the crowd's continued positive exclamations. His voice now carried a higher level of energy. "It's good news today . . . the good news is that you can find salvation in Christ alone. Salvation is not to be found in the rituals of the church. Not in the Roman church, not in Zwingli's Gross Muenster you see behind me." He turned and gestured toward the church. "It's in faith and clinging to Jesus, this is what I've learned. You can see from my dress, I'm a monk from Saint Lucius monastery. I am intimate with the church, but today we will not speak of that. We will speak of Christ alone and a life anchored in Him, a life that comes from Him."

Jorg continued expounding on the love of Christ and how it had changed his life. When he finished, Conrad slapped him on the back. "Good job. I feel like a proud father."

"But I am older than you; you can't be my father," Jorg said with a big smile.

"No matter, I am proud."

Because of the size of the crowd and the excitement of Jorg's first time preaching, Conrad and Jorg didn't notice two friends in the crowd. One was Remy, restlessly walking the city, still with a slight limp. He stopped to watch and nodded his head at Jorg. He wasn't certain he believed in Jorg's God, but the crowd did, and they loved him. The other friend was Anna, who also stopped to listen to the monk from the church. She watched and listened intently. She heard Jorg call it good news, and it was to her. She took it with her that day. It rested on her and felt healing.

❧

Chapter 14

At that evening's gathering at Jakob and Priscilla's, Conrad stood beside Jorg, his hand on Jorg's shoulder. "You should have seen old Jorg here," he declared to the room.

Jorg cast Conrad a half-amused, sideways smile. "Old Jorg?" he said.

Conrad continued, "It was his first time preaching and it was well received by those gathered." With a look of pride, Conrad returned a sideways look toward Jorg. "In all seriousness, people were touched by what our friend here had to say. He simply used his story, and what a powerful one it is. One man told us afterward that he and his friend wondered what to expect, seeing a monk in a robe preaching. Would he speak against the council and encourage the people to turn the city back to the Roman church? The man said they were drawn to Jorg, and when they understood what he was about, they were challenged to consider their ways."

Jakob spoke up. "I don't think we know Jorg's full story. You should soon speak your story out to the gathering at the guild, brother."

Jorg nodded and replied in his booming voice, "I am ready and willing to do that."

Barbara gestured toward the table. "Let's gather around, it's time to eat."

After eating and laughing together, they remembered the Lord around the large table as was their custom.

Then Jakob said, "I want to welcome Jorg and Remy," and nodded to them. "We rejoice in Jorg joining our two brothers, Conrad and Felix, in speaking to those who are looking for God's healing in their lives. Welcome to you. Now, tonight will be a little different. We will hear again from one of the sisters. Priscilla, please speak your heart."

Priscilla took a deep breath and smiled at Barbara. Knowing she was among friends, she began. She taught on a bible passage from the Gospel of John that she had studied for years but had never taught on. When she finished there was a moment of quiet as the group took in what she had shared. Because the pause was so long, she began doubting her choice of subject, thinking possibly they didn't care for it. Then the group broke out into animated conversation, everyone talking at once.

Priscilla looked at Barbara and saw her expression of joy. Jorg, with a smile that spread from ear to ear, talked excitedly to anyone who would listen. Jakob looked at Priscilla with pride and affirmation, and she breathed out.

"Good word, daughter!"

"We will have to hear more from you," Conrad added.

Jakob said, "Why don't you and Jorg give what God is speaking to you at the next guild meeting?"

As the meeting ended, Jorg approached Jakob. "What your daughter spoke of tonight fits well with my story. It answered a question that has weighed heavily on me since I was at the monastery."

"Very good. We will hear it at the next meeting. I look forward to it," Jakob said.

Remy held back most of the night. He came because, after his conversation with his father, he felt a sense of not being of use. Seeing his opportunity, he approached Jakob. "Master Jakob," he said, "about the cobbling, sir. I wanted to ask what your plans for me are. I hope to start soon." He searched Jakob's face.

"Let us meet tomorrow at the guild hall and we will talk."

"Tomorrow then," Remy said, with new hope.

Arriving at the hall the next morning, Remy found himself surrounded by the noise of many looms. He had only been to the guild for meetings and was surprised at the transformation of the area during the workday. The four apprentices looked up at him as he entered. This made him feel out of place.

"Is Master Jakob about?" he asked. He was pointed to the back area. Remy passed by an apprentice who was receiving instructions. From the tenor of the instruction, he could tell the youth must be a beginner, and he thought of his own new beginning. He found Jakob looking over an area in the back.

"What do you think, Remy? Will this be enough room for your work?"

"It looks like it will do. There's space to hang tools and room to work."

"And you have the equipment needed?" Jakob asked.

"Yes. I have the basic needs. It is what I worked with before when I cobbled, back before I joined the peasant armies. My father will be pleased that I am at it again. He has told me as much."

"Making shoes for those in need is a preferable undertaking to making war, I believe," Jakob said, looking again at the space.

"I believe the cause of the peasants to be an honorable one," Remy said, taking offense at Jakob's remark. "They are resisting their unfair treatment by the landlords. Much has been taken from them. Many were forced off their properties, and some have lost everything. They are hardworking people. I have noticed the brethren have a great passion for their cause, for what you believe. Is that not true? Are we not alike in that?" Remy said heatedly.

Jakob heard the fire and suffering in Remy's voice and his head shot up.

Remy continued, "You and your men should consider taking your cause to the battlefield if you believe in that cause. We Swiss are known as fierce fighters."

Jakob, realizing that he had offended the young man, said kindly, "Yes, we are alike, you and I, and yet different."

Remy went on, "And your cause, your doctrines, your creeds, are they not worth the shedding of blood?"

"I hear what you are saying, Remy, but we will not fight brother against brother for we all believe in the same Lord. We will not take up the sword against those in control. We fight with the Word of God. I would hope that those under my influence would never take up arms. This is not our way; we are people of peace. We speak peace and pray for peace."

Remi shook his head. He didn't understand these people. But he thought it best to move on.

Chapter 15

*Where children wandering wearily
have not yet found their home*

Conrad and Jorg were making their way to the front of the crowd when someone yelled out, "Here comes Strong Jorg!" Cheers broke out and someone began calling his name like a chant. When they reached the church steps, Jorg turned to face Conrad, who laughed and slapped him on the back. "You're becoming a crowd favorite," he said.

Jorg faced the crowd, a smile blazing across his face. As he marveled at the size of it, he saw the young woman who had been at the guild meeting. He had thought of her as a lost and wandering soul that night. As he began to speak, he thought of the crowd as those who wandered and were lost.

Anna listened, face upturned, and she heard the message. But then an impression came to her, and she realized she needed to return home. Walking down the cobblestones, she felt an urgency and picked up her pace. Entering the back door of the large house, she greeted the cook who cast her the usual disparaging look, then spit out, "Father Fredrik is looking for you."

Anna's stomach tensed and she thought, *What is coming?*

At that moment Fredrik burst into the room. "What do you know about the cat I found?" He stared suspiciously at her. "Follow me," he commanded. He led her through the house and out the front door. There she saw the little kitten, waiting in a cage. It whimpered and stared up at her with eyes that once again sought a savior. Not wanting this trouble or what was to come, Anna stood silently, looking at the little one she loved so entirely.

"Is this yours? I found it wandering around the house. It is, isn't it?" he hissed, his face coming close to hers. "Well, not anymore. I won't have it on my property."

A cry of pain came from deep within Anna. Everything had been taken from her. Her unborn babies with Fredrik and now the kitten. Not caring what Fredrik thought, she turned, ran out the door, and rushed toward the guild. She needed comfort, and she knew she would find it there.

Fredrik, standing in the doorway called after her: "Where are you going? You will never see this creature again. You should say goodbye to it!" Then he slammed the door.

Walking briskly toward the guild and the meeting there, Anna had time to think. *How unhappy she was so much of the time in her life with Fredrik.* She pictured her little kitten in the cage with its big, pleading eyes. "I feel like I live in a cage," she whispered to herself. "How could Fredrik treat that poor, defenseless animal like that?" There were times he had no heart. She pictured herself the day she rescued the kitten. *How vulnerable it had been!* She breathed a deep sigh. She stayed there in the moment remembering the kitten.

Turning the corner, she saw the guild at the end of the street. *What if she left Fredrik—for good?* She mulled this over. *Could that even work? Where would she go?* She thought about the hateful look on his face; it made her shiver. He had such power over her. *No, there was no escape.* She stopped outside the guildhall and thought of her plight for a moment. Then she sighed and opened the door to the hall and the noise of the gathering. She felt the contrast between the joy in the room and her melancholy.

Feeling the weight of what had just happened, Anna sat in a chair in a corner. She took in the activity in the room with little energy on her part and, to her surprise, little interest in taking part. Yet she wanted to be invited to do so. She felt lonely. *Had she been mistaken in thinking she fit in with this group?*

Barbara approached her. "Anna, why don't you join us? Priscilla and I are watching the game."

Anna shook her head and looked away. She watched the game of pick-up sticks being played and wished she was a part of it. But when an acquaintance from the last meeting, a young woman with long dark hair who was actively playing, asked her to play, she shook her head again, despite yearning to be a part of the fun. Then the acquaintance approached her again. "Play with us, Anna. You seem discouraged." She looked sympathetically at Anna. "Play with us. It will take your mind off your troubles." She begged and reached out her hand. Anna shook her head.

"Come on," the friend repeated, pleading.

Anna wanted to have someone plead with her, she had hoped for that. "All right, but I want you to know I haven't played this game in forever," Anna said to her.

"It will come back to you again, I promise," the woman said.

Anna looked at the extended hand and put her hand there. She joined in. And as her acquaintance had said, it came back to her.

Jakob, having broken away from a conversation with Felix and Conrad, stood to get everyone's attention. "Friends, let us welcome someone who has not yet spoken in our meetings. You may know him. He's been preaching with some who are more familiar, Felix and Conrad." Jakob gestured toward them. "Come forth, brother Jorg."

Jorg stepped up and began in with his big voice, "Brothers and sisters, I am Jorg of the House of Jakob. Some of you have met me but others do not know my full story. Master Jakob has asked me to share tonight so I will. I have come from the monastery of Saint Lucian. I was a monk there. And, although I was committed to a life of holiness, I was a man with no peace," he said. He paused, looked around, and settled on Anna, who had her head down. He continued, "During the times of silence at the monastery, a phrase came to me. From that time on I was plagued with the thought, the question. It stayed with me day and night. I couldn't escape the way it burned into my being. It haunted me, and it wasn't until I surrendered that I found an answer." Jorg stopped, as if reliving his experiences.

"And the question, brother?" said Jakob, his eyes wide with interest.

"There were two questions. First: 'What is truth?' Later the question, 'How should I then live?' I saw good brothers in the monastery, but I also saw corruption and the love of money and possessions. Some brothers even had concubines or lovers. I felt stained, tormented. A time came when I could bear it no longer. I had to leave, but where should I go? I knew my family would not welcome me. They were set on my becoming a priest. I heard what was happening here in Zurich, so I walked out one day and kept walking. I listened to the preachers in the town square, whom I now know to be Conrad and Felix," he said, nodding toward them. They heartily acknowledged him. "At one point I found myself at a church here in Zurich, my heart in such turmoil and so broken. I repented there."

The crowd grew quiet as he continued.

"I knew I was on the right path because I began to feel peace. More and more peace. The darkness that had hung over me for months, years really, began to lessen. But it wasn't until attending a gathering at the home of our friend Conrad that I received the answers for which I was looking. After my time of sorrow, I didn't expect what I came to experience. Joy sprang up in me, something I had never hoped to know. This came from an unexpected source . . . through the voice of a woman. God used someone I didn't expect to be used—someone you all know, the guild master's daughter, Priscilla."

Everyone looked at Priscilla. She felt stunned by his comment and uncomfortable with the attention.

Jakob spoke up. "Daughter, will you share with us the word you gave that night?"

She gave the message she had the previous night, from the gospel of John on "Thy word is truth," weaving it together with Jesus proclaiming he was "the Way, the Truth, and the Life." It was well received by the group, and Priscilla felt a sense of relief, a burden falling from her shoulders.

Afterward, Barbara took Priscilla's hand. "That was wonderful," she said. "I've never heard a message quite like it until you gave it. Hearts were touched. I know mine was! Good job, sister."

"What do you think Anna thought? She seemed so sad when she came in," Priscilla said.

"She did, didn't she? I saw the younger woman invite her to join in the game. I think it helped her."

"Yes. I thought it wonderful that they insisted she play with them. I've wondered at times if Anna's childhood was stolen from her."

"She told me she played that game as a small girl," Barbara said. "I enjoyed watching her laughing." They glanced at Anna, with her new friends sitting beside her. Anna saw them and gave Barbara and Priscilla a big smile.

Just then, Priscilla felt someone standing beside her. Turning, she saw it was William. He towered over her as she noted how handsome he was with his curly hair, a gray one or two, and brown eyes.

"I was inspired by the messages tonight, especially yours, Priscilla," he said kindly.

"Thank you, sir. You should come more often. Others have even more inspiring words to impart. I am only a beginner."

"I think not," William said. "You seem to have a deep source from which you drink."

"Thank you again for your kind words." She nodded, seeing something new in his eyes she hadn't seen before. After he walked away, Barbara said, "A councilman with encouraging words for our group, that's a new occurrence."

"Not really. William has been coming off and on. He has in the past defended us before the council."

Barbara raised her eyebrows. "He seemed to have a keen interest in you."

Priscilla shook her head. "Oh, don't be ridiculous. Why would you say that?"

Barbara considered this and smiled. "Back to the councilman's interest in our meetings," she said. "I'm surprised. Maybe Jakob is right. Perhaps we will win their hearts. This brings something to mind I have failed to mention. Conrad says the council members are no longer interfering with them as they preach."

"That's encouraging," Priscilla said, as Anna came up beside her.

"Priscilla, may I talk with you?"

"Of course."

"Could we meet tomorrow privately?"

"Yes, come to my home and we'll talk. Is everything all right?"

Anna didn't answer.

Chapter 16

Priscilla stood at the window, watching and worrying. *How dreary and dark it is these days. Where is the sun?* The weather had been similar the day she and Jakob saw Anna save the endangered kitten. Seeing Anna outside, Priscilla hurried to the door. She got Anna settled in a chair. Looking into her eyes Priscilla knew something was very wrong.

Priscilla sat back in her chair. "What is the matter, dear child?"

Anna took a deep breath. "Oh, Priscilla, I must speak of something today that is very hard for me to say. After hearing Jorg and you speak last night, I knew I had to talk to you. The truth needs to come out." With her head bowed low, Anna said, "I have a confession to make."

Priscilla sat forward in her chair, close to Anna, wondering where she was with her faith. "Would you not confess to your parish priest?" Seeing the distress on Anna's face, she immediately regretted her words.

"Oh no, I can't confess to him." She looked at Priscilla with a tormented expression. "It's about him." Tears formed in the corners of her eyes and fell on her hands clasped tightly in her lap. "It's about him . . . and about my sin."

Priscilla felt herself begin to tighten up in her back and her neck. She sat back in the chair and imagined different possibilities. She felt herself wanting to condemn the young woman before her, but she hoped not to go there.

Anna began, "It was about this time of the year that I came to live at our priest's house. I was fourteen years old and had lost my parents and brothers to sickness. My aunt was the housekeeper at Father Fredrik's home. She invited me to come to work with her. She said I should feel honored and grateful to live in a great man's home. And I was, Priscilla, I was." She looked away. "I was a devout young girl, one who looked forward to mass. I would kneel before the crucifix in the church, and I loved the One who hung there. When I was older, maybe fifteen, Father Fredrik took it upon himself to teach me to read."

Anna's face became animated. "I was very excited, Priscilla. You can imagine, can't you? For me, an orphan and a peasant to be able to read! How would I ever be able to do so without his care? I was a good student. Fredrik was proud of me, he told me so." Anna smiled, tilted her head, and continued. "We would laugh together but then. . . ." Suddenly, her smile was gone. "One day he said to me, 'Today we will do something different.' He said he wanted me to come to his bedchamber."

Anna stared at the wall for a moment. "I was so young and frightened that night, I was trembling. I had been taught to obey without question. He showed me a glass of red wine and asked, 'Have you ever tasted wine? ' I shook my head. He said, 'Taste it' and stood watching me drink. It was very sweet and made me sleepy." Anna's eyes pleaded with Priscilla. For a moment Priscilla thought of the little kitten and wondered what she would say.

"Later, I woke up in his bed. I asked myself what had happened. This was the beginning of my sin, our sin." Anna was quiet for a while. She looked down. "Winter came to my soul then. There was no one to help me. I thought, shouldn't my aunt come to my rescue? Instead, she began to look at me with a mixture of sadness and disgust. I felt orphaned anew. None saw my sorrow and I couldn't turn to God, He seemed far away. I felt condemned." She looked at Priscilla, her eyes pleading again, "Do you condemn me?"

Priscilla felt unsure of what to say. "You were so young, the priest misused you, Anna." Those were the words that came out of her mouth, but she couldn't halt her feelings of accusation.

Anna looked at Priscilla, unsure she could trust what she had said.

Priscilla wondered if Anna had heard the doubt in her voice.

Anna jumped up from the chair. "This is too much! I can't say more. Maybe tomorrow. I've got to go now." She rushed to the door and was outside before Priscilla could stop her.

Priscilla was shocked to her core. She had no idea how long she sat thinking until she heard her father walk into the room.

"Whatever has happened, Priscilla? You are as pale as if you have seen some great tragedy."

"It's Anna. Sit here and I'll tell you what I know. I need your wisdom today."

After hearing the story, Jakob was incensed. "It was wrong of that man to have used her that way." Priscilla could see his anger, an anger she rarely saw in her father.

"It was hard for me to hear her story. Yes, he was wrong, but she stays with him. And I'm feeling a battle in my heart: I condemn her, yet my heart goes out to her. Back and forth. It's a war within me between mercy and judgment, and I am concerned that judgment is winning."

"We are not to be the accuser of the brethren. We must never take that part," her father said.

"It's a heartbreaking story; I'm certain we haven't heard the end of it. I must prepare myself," Priscilla said.

The next day, Anna returned. Priscilla pulled her chair close to Anna and said kindly, "Please feel free to continue with your story today."

"This has been very hard for me, but I feel a little less burdened after yesterday." Anna sighed and smiled weakly at Priscilla. "Are you certain that what I have confessed doesn't cause you to feel disdain for me? Are you disgusted when you look at me?"

"No child, by God's grace, I am not." Priscilla prayed that God would help her.

Anna continued, "I have been so divided, Priscilla. The shame I bear it's like a heavy blanket I wear on my shoulders, an unbearable weight." At this, she crossed her arms before her. "Yet I have felt pride that I have lived in the home of this great man. It is a beautiful home, and I was proud that I shared Fredrik's life. I shared his pain and disappointment when he was demoted, and his big church taken from him. I told him he was a great man still. One night, in his bed, he spoke of Zwingli and other reformers and how they were changing his world. This conversation lit a strange fire in me. Who was this Zwingli, himself a former priest, I had heard? By then, I could read well, so when my household chores were finished, I would go to Fredrik's library to look for a book about the reformers. But there I found a bible, and a door was opened to me. Shortly afterward I found you, Priscilla, and the others, and for that I am very grateful."

Priscilla patted Anna's hand and smiled reassuringly. "Is there more?"

"I have come to realize that although I have felt something of a wife to Fredrik, I am not," Anna said sadly. "We are called concubines and other priests have them." Her eyes darkened. "During those years I twice found myself with child. When this happened, I was told I must take an herbal drink to take care of my problem. I had some pain, and it was over. But the pain was replaced by sadness. I had dreamed of a child to share joy with, but it was not to be. I became the motherless child and the childless mother." Her eyes darted back and forth.

Hearing this, Priscilla's mother's heart cried out at the pain she saw in Anna.

"And now a change has come over Fredrik. He drinks heavily. There was a time when he would speak to me with tender, loving words. But now he will sometimes call me a poor beggar, blessed to have him for a benefactor, and then says I am undeserving of him. And I see how he looks at some of the young girls and fear fills my heart. He has said to me, 'I'm going to find another lover.' I am all alone in the world, I have no family. What would happen to me if I am cast out?"

"You are not alone, Anna. You have my father and me and the others. If you need to leave, you will have a home, we will see to it."

"Well, there's one more thing . . . something I haven't told anyone." She paused. "I am with child again."

Chapter 17

"What will you do, Anna?" Priscilla asked calmly. Hesitating, and looking like she would burst into tears, Anna said, "I will have to tell him. I want this baby, Priscilla. I won't give it up, but I want Fredrik also. He has always taken care of me . . . in a way." She looked at Priscilla with uncertainty. "And I love him, despite the past, and how he has treated me," Anna said.

Anna hesitated outside the library door for a long time. The housekeeper walked by, casting a suspicious look her way, and then went on to some chore in another part of the house. Still, Anna didn't knock. She remembered the first time she'd walked into Fredrik's library, when she was very young and new to the house. That night she had taken a candle in hand, and she stood in awe in the doorway for a moment. A room full of books. She peeked both ways down the hall to make sure no one had seen her. When she knew she was safe, she walked in and picked up one of the books. It was to her like a great, wonderful treasure chest with a beautiful ornate lock. She couldn't read yet, but just being able to hold the book with its fine gilding, the smell of the paper, and the look of the script was enough for her at that moment.

That was another time, long ago. Today she stood in the open doorway looking at Fredrik. He was bent over his desk, too involved in his work to notice her. He was writing something, maybe a homily. Now, there she was with the same words that had caused so much trouble before. She realized she should take courage and prayed to the Lord for help.

Finally, he looked up. "What do you want?" he said brusquely.

She paused, unsure of if he wanted her to come farther into the room. That was settled when he said, "Come in, then." With her heart pounding, she walked across the old wooden floor, creaking with age, telling its story. Now she would have to tell hers.

"What is it, can't you see I'm busy?" he said, looking down again at his work.

She waited. When he looked up, she said quickly, while she still had the courage, "I have something to tell you. I believe I'm with child."

He looked at her, a look she wasn't sure how to interpret. She thought it was a look of pain, impatience, anger, or possibly something else. "You will have to take care of that," he said without feeling.

"Fredrik, we could hide it, no one need know, it will be our secret." She knew this was a ridiculous thing to say. It was her desperation speaking, desperation fueled by past disappointment.

He left the desk, came close to her, and began to raise his voice. Then, remembering the housekeeper, he quieted. Stepping even closer, he said in a menacing way, "We will not have a child in this house. I am a priest and there will be no more conversation about this. I don't want anyone to know, do you understand?"

Courage sprang up in her. "It is your child also. Do you feel no remorse, Fredrik?" When there was no response, she said, "I beg you, Fredrik. Don't take this child from me. I cannot bear to lose a child again."

"You will do as I say." He walked back to his chair, shooed her away with his hand, and put his head down as if nothing had transpired between them.

A sense of utter dejection fell upon her. The library, once a treasure of wonders, now took on a different presence.

Later that night, as Anna lay in bed she thought about Priscilla. Why was she fighting this battle alone? She had opened her heart to Priscilla, who had shown herself a friend. With that thought, Anna determined to share this with her, and she felt better, and the darkness she felt broke.

Later that week, when she could get away, Anna walked to Priscilla's home. "Fredrik treats me differently now. So cold. Sometimes I feel I need to leave. But his home has been mine for so long that when I think of leaving it feels like I'm jumping off a cliff into a dark cavern."

"Anna, I don't think you know what is within you," Priscilla said. "I want to encourage you to reach deep into God. The strength you need is there. Trust God in this. Take your time. When the time is right you will be ready, and we will help you in any way we can. And of course, I will pray for you."

Later that evening, the thought that she must protect the baby sounded through Anna's mind. Strength and resolve arose in her; she felt herself a fierce lioness. *There must be an answer.* After the others were in bed, she took a candle into the library, looking for something, unsure of what it might be. Sitting down with the candle flickering, she opened the big ornate bible to scripture she had found the day before.

Now she found something fresh. While the candle flame danced, she bent low to the bible to read the words: "I lift up my eyes to the hills—where does my help come from?" She thought about the hills surrounding the city. "My help comes from the Lord, the Maker of heaven and earth. He will not let your foot slip—He who watches over you will not slumber . . . The Lord watches over you—the Lord is your shade at your right hand; the sun will not harm you by day, nor the moon by night. The Lord will keep you from all harm—He will watch over your life; the Lord will watch over your coming and going both now and forevermore."

The psalm spoke to Anna. The Lord would watch over them both—the baby, and her. At that moment, her fear dropped away, and a thought came. *Or was it hope?* Priscilla had offered help. But somehow, in her fear and tension, Anna had forgotten. Priscilla could be her way out, the salvation she needed.

This thought felt a taste and a wisp of freedom—a little feather of hope that floated into her being. It was a soft and delicate one, but nevertheless a hope. It fed something new in her: a yearning for a different life. She hadn't dared think of such a thing. Hope took away her fear and nourished her.

She knew what she would do.

Chapter 18

What though the tumult
of the storm increase

Anna was afraid. She picked up her pace. The city was dark as she walked. She had heard the rumors of people being accosted by bandits. She glanced over her shoulder as she hurried along the rough cobblestone streets. She tripped several times, righted herself, and moved on. She seldom had the need to be out in the city this late. But tonight was different; she felt alone and abandoned. This propelled her on.

Earlier, she had hastily packed her belongings into a small bag and waited for Fredrik and the housekeeper to fall asleep. Wrapping a cloak around her shoulders, she fled into the unwelcoming darkness. Her passage took her by many homes. In a window or two, she saw shimmering candles and imagined the homeowners' cozy, happy lives. Maybe someday that would be her life.

She reached her destination. Standing before the door, she remembered the library door and the disappointment she had experienced. But this was Jakob and Priscilla's door, and she knocked with hope. She waited. No response. She started to breathe hard. Her heart pounded. It was late. Of course, they were asleep. It was probably a mistake to arrive at this hour. What should she do? She didn't feel comfortable walking the streets with the dangers there. She knocked louder. Just as she began to panic, the door opened a crack. There was Priscilla, holding a candle.

"Anna, it's so dark, I didn't recognize you. You've been crying. Come in out of the cold. Are you all right?"

Speaking with trepidation, Anna said, "Does your offer still stand? Am I welcome tonight?"

"You are, of course, welcome. Have you left him?"

Anna nodded.

"Then you must stay for as long as you need."

Anna felt an overwhelming sense of relief. She was welcome. Had she ever been welcomed? She couldn't remember if she had.

❧

The next day Anna and Greta worked together to clean the kitchen after the meal. Priscilla had tried to talk Anna out of it, but Anna was insistent. She and Greta chatted merrily as they worked. Priscilla and Jakob sat around a roaring fire listening to their banter and discussed Anna's decision.

"I'm proud of her," Priscilla said. "She's very brave to take this action. Father Fredrik was quite abusive. He wanted to control her in every way he could."

"You told her we are happy to welcome her, didn't you?"

"Yes, she knows," Priscilla said. "She said scripture was her encouragement."

Jakob nodded and smiled. "She will be safe here. We will see to it. By the way, the young preachers tell me they haven't heard much from the council lately. I said I hadn't heard from them either. It's puzzling. What do you think, daughter?"

"'Tis puzzling. I wonder if William would have some insight?"

The council had been silent for some weeks, but the Brotherhood had not heard the last from them.

The next afternoon Jakob, Priscilla, and Anna sat finishing their dinner when a knock came at the door. It was Katrina's oldest son, asking Priscilla to come and attend to one of the other children. She packed up some herbs and left.

After attending to the child and having a bit of shared conversation with Katrina, Priscilla glanced out the window. "Look how late it is, I must get home. I'm certain this remedy will be effective for the little one," she said warmly to Katrina. They said their goodbyes and Priscilla started down the street.

Thinking of the late hour, and remembering talking with Anna about bandits, she thought perhaps she should have asked her father to accompany her. Just then, she thought she saw someone in the shadows, standing near a house close to the street. But as she passed that spot, there was no one there. She breathed a sigh of relief. To be safe, she picked up her gait. Then she heard footsteps behind her. With a beating heart, she walked faster. But the footsteps quickened as well. She hurried on. Knowing she was being followed, panic seized her. Block by block, house by house, whoever it was, was getting closer. *It must be a man! How could she outpace him?*

She didn't dare turn around for fear of slowing down. She was winded. How long could she keep up this pace? Nearly running, she heard her pursuer running as well. Then she felt this person, a robber possibly, very close to her. Too close. She wheeled around. And came face to face with Bruno Heinrich, the magistrate.

"What are you doing out alone at night?" he said with stony coldness. "Attending births?"

She stood still for a moment, paralyzed with fear at the expression in his eyes. Then she turned and rushed away.

Priscilla sat in her chair, her bible in her lap. A flickering candle and a cup of herbal tea sat on the table beside her. She watched the steam waft up from the cup and patted the bible, but her mind was elsewhere. Her thoughts were on one thing only: the actions of the magistrate on the previous night. Her father's comments seemed plausible. He'd said he thought the councilmembers were changing their tactics. After a break, they were once again taking up the harassment of the brethren. She knew she should have felt peace here at home with her bible, but she had to admit she was struggling with anxiety and fear.

The magistrate had been so close last night, so hateful. She had felt his very breath. It was unnerving, unexpected, and frightening. The bible went unattended. Today, her thoughts and fears ruled her.

Chapter 19

Sparks danced about the wood in the fireplace, floating and flickering gaily, as if happy to be released. The fireplace warmth was delicious to Anna. It was so often cold at Fredrik's, but tonight she felt the kindness of Jakob and Priscilla's home. At the rectory, there was always a tension, one she never understood. Here, for the first time, she felt safe and welcome. She had dreamed of belonging and here she had found it amongst friends.

But there was one thing she didn't know what to do with. Something she struggled over: she thought she still loved Fredrik. It made no sense after all that had happened, but she couldn't push it aside. She wrestled with it the rest of the evening. Later, getting ready for bed, a familiar heaviness fell upon her. It was a battle she had known before, and it had its grip upon her again. She knew it was wrong for her to continue the relationship with Fredrik. Her new sense of God spoke to her, and she knew the relationship was sin . . .

but she loved him. The darkness within grew. Finally, in desperation, she prayed before she went to sleep: "How can I find peace? Lord, help me."

Waking with a start the next morning, she sat up in bed. Jakob would have an answer for her. She knew it.

Jakob sat meditating quietly over scripture. He heard the sound of footsteps and looked up to see Anna pulling up a chair to sit beside him.

"Anna," he said affectionately.

"How do you get there?" she said.

"What do you mean, child?"

"I feel my sin, Papa." She used Priscilla's affectionate name for her father. "It's heavy upon me, I can find no relief," she sighed.

"Oh, I see." He sat quietly, looking for words. Peering up at her, he said, "You must go to the Lord, confess, and turn from your sin. He will make a way for you to come to a place of peace. That's what you want, don't you, Anna? A place of peace."

She nodded.

"To be relieved of our burdens, we must go to the Lord. Only He can set us free. The practice of religion cannot do it, only He can. Do you know He loves you, Anna?"

"I feel His love sometimes," she said, barely above a whisper.

"And you have asked Him into your heart?"

She nodded again.

"Good, that's a start." Jakob smiled at her. "He calls us to Himself, and He says in scripture, 'Come all who are heavy laden,' and He promises to give us rest. You say you have burdens?"

Her eyes begged for relief.

"Speak that out to Him, speak your need, and then be still. Wait for Him and He will answer your prayer. He is faithful. He is within our hearts, He's not far away as some think, He's very near. Does that make sense to you, dear Anna?"

"I feel unworthy of Him."

"We are all unworthy of His love and forgiveness, Anna." Jakob reached over to touch her hand. "That is the story. None of us has the right to come into His presence, none are worthy. Yet He has made a way for us to come. His presence dwells within us, here, in our hearts." Jakob tapped his chest.

"He is calling you to go deeper. It's His delight to spend time with you and eventually, it will become your joy also."

"This is what I want, Papa."

"Behold Him. Sit alone with Him and enjoy His presence. If you do this, He will become more real to you. Your peace will come. And you will see that He bears our burdens upon himself. Would you like to pray together now?"

"I would."

***

Conrad looked with interest at the group of young peasant men circling Remy at the guild hall. He moved closer to learn more. His eyes were drawn to Remy. He saw that he had the body of a soldier, well-built and powerful, and he observed a purposefulness about Remy that made men want to follow him. Those that circled him were very engaged and looked at him with admiration. Conrad had never seen Remy so energized.

Then Jorg approached Remy from the side. Conrad heard Jorg say, his expression fierce, "Why are you talking about fighting and the peasant wars when you know the brethren are pacifists? This meeting is about God, not war."

"It's history and they keep asking me questions about it!" Remy said, standing his ground. "If you don't like the conversation move to another part of the room."

Conrad watched Jorg move away.

One of the young men said, "Tell us about the pikemen."

"Yes! The pikemen were Swiss soldiers who were unbeatable in battle." Remy attempted to lower his voice but, in his excitement, it got louder. "They would form a tight square of men holding seven-foot-tall pikes. Marching in that square they would charge the enemy. They were swift and could cover ground in an unbelievably brief time. Before the enemy could set his own position, the pikemen were on him." The young men stood in awe, encouraging him.

"Small groups of these pikemen could prevail and cause great damage, even to those on horseback. In the Swabian War . . . have you heard of it?"

They nodded, eager for more.

"In that war, six hundred men of Zurich were caught in the open plain by one thousand Austrian soldiers—on horseback, mind you." With an intense look Remy went on, "They formed what was called the Hedgehog, the tightly formed square I mentioned." He watched for their affirmation, and they were eager to give it. "They easily defeated that large army. The Swiss were swift, and they persisted because they were not overloaded with armor.

"Then there were the halberds," Remy continued, taking a moment to allow his listeners to catch up to him. "With that long weapon, with its sharp threatening blade at the end, a man on the ground could take an armored man down, pulling him off his horse by piercing his armor. Now picture this!" Remy paused dramatically ". . . the Hapsburg knights, now hear me, they were the best the Hapsburgs could offer! They were mounted on horseback," he said, emphasizing *horseback*, "mounted and in armor and they were taken down, defeated by these pikemen."

The young men began to cheer, as others around them looked on in surprise and curiosity.

As Remy continued to hold forth, Conrad, knowing Felix was scheduled to speak that night, approached Jakob. "Master Jakob, I have something burning on my heart. I know that it is Felix's night, but would I be allowed to share a little?"

"Yes, brother, you go first then."

Conrad got the attention of the group. "I have been listening to our brother Remy speak of his experiences, and maybe some others have listened as well. He has done a service, reminding us who we are. We have had a great many people come up against us lately, and fear has arisen in our midst. Remy has reminded us that we are Swiss and are indeed a strong and valiant people with a long history of opposing enemies greater than us.

"Now we must remember that people are not our enemy, for we wrestle not against flesh and blood. The council is not our enemy. But let me remind you that we Swiss are people of steadfast courage and fervent self-sacrifice. We must remember this during this time. Remy, you mentioned oath brothers. I hope we will be that to each other, sharing together, and praying for each other. We must remember to keep this in mind. It is who we are and who we have been in the past. We have always been a people who encouraged each other, stood together and helped those around us. This spoke to me. We must not let the pressure of the council break us! We must continue to stand together. Let us remember this. Let us love one another. We do battle, yes, but we battle with the truth. We spread the truth in love, that is our greatest weapon."

Jorg stood outside the guild hall that day calling people in. "I cry out like Saint John the Baptist, 'Repent, for the Kingdom of God draws near.' Hear me now, you who rail against the wealthy landowners and the merchants. Yes, they rob you. Yes, the church asks for tithes, too much for the plowman, the workers. I ask you to stop and consider something. What profit will you gain if you were to win this fight, yet your soul is not right with God? I have a story to tell: I was a man with everything—wealth, prestige, all of it. I gave up everything for the monastery, but I had no peace until I found the Lord. Repent of your hatred toward the landowners! Repent and be set free! Come inside and we will talk."

Many who came in were new to the Brotherhood. One man, a plowman named Josef, was especially engaged and came afterward to talk to Jakob. "You are right to speak to these people about these things. My people are peasants. They are needy, they have lost much. Their hearts are open to a new way to freedom. My friends and neighbors have had experience with heartache, and the burden of hatred weighs heavily on them. It adds to their burden of poverty and want. They are searching for something more. You should visit us in the town of Waldshut and speak more to them. I have warned them about rising up against the nobles and the landowners. Some vow to go to war again. I am but one voice. They would listen to you. Please consider coming to Waldshut. Your voice would be heard there."

The next day marked a new beginning for Conrad and Barbara. In contrast to the tensions in the city, delight and joy came to them. Their baby was born.

Jorg and Remy looked down at the baby and Remy said, "Look at that, Jorg, she took hold of my finger. Did you know they were this small, babies I mean?"

"What's her name, Remy?"

"Issabella, I told you that was her name."

Jorg ignored the jab and leaned forward to coo at the baby. "Look at her, I think she understands me, she's smiling."

"She's not smiling at you, you oaf." Remy poked Jorg in the ribs.

The baby started to cry.

"What's wrong? Why do you think she is crying?" Jorg looked at Remy with alarm.

"You probably scared her with that face of yours," Remy said with a slight smile.

"No, she just wants her mother," Barbara said, hurrying in from the kitchen. She picked up the baby. Turning toward Remy and Jorg, she said, "It's dinner time."

Chapter 20

Priscilla knew her father had been put in a position he didn't want to be in. His only desire was to practice his faith quietly and be an encourager to others. But the young men had changed that private faith to one that shouted, "Listen, hear this: consider your lives, turn, and believe." Now the council had turned against Jakob, and he had determined long ago never to make an enemy of a brother in Christ. He viewed the council members as such. Yet now, it seemed he had become their enemy. If only the young men had used a little diplomacy!

Priscilla watched her father drum his fingers on the table. Wanting to encourage the one who had taken the place of encourager so often in her life, she said, "You have been on the council for many years, Papa, and have always been well respected in this city. Surely they will listen this time."

He silenced his fingers. "Thank you, Priscilla. I must appeal to them one more time. Perhaps it will be possible to reconcile. I will go tomorrow."

The magistrate glared at Jakob, who sat before him. "Master Jakob, what is this about your people stirring up the peasants? We all know the dangers, they could foment a rebellion. More peasant wars are a possibility, I'm sure you agree. Until now, Zurich has been free of the upheaval seen in other cantons of Switzerland. What have you to say about your people's influence upon the peasants? My special concern is Felix Manz."

Jakob weighed Heinrich's words. He had not come prepared to discuss this. He hoped to be a peacemaker. He hoped the magistrate would consider the youth and inexperience of the young men. Jakob was aware of the council's low opinion of Felix—both because of his birth circumstances and his determination to continue preaching despite their warnings and threats. Could he win the magistrate over today?

As Jakob considered these things, the magistrate broke into his thoughts. "Manz continues to print lies in those broadsides that he reads to the crowds. This stirs them up all the more."

"Felix is a man of peace. I know it is not his intention to stir the people up."

"But it is happening, isn't it?" the magistrate objected. "The peasants are enraged. We see this as your young men speak in front of the old church—*Zwingli's church*. Huldrich Zwingli is unhappy with the peasants and others gathering there. Think about it, Master Jakob. How might Zwingli feel? It is our aim in this city to maintain order. We have only recently taken control from the Catholics. What would happen if, in the chaos of a peasant uprising, the Catholics took the city back?" The magistrate frowned at Jakob and his voice rose. "It is my job to keep the peace, is it not?" He pounded the table. "I think we are done here!"

Jakob had come to beg forgiveness for the young men's bravado. But the magistrate was not amenable, and Jakob was convinced he would not change. Discouraged, he prepared to leave when Heinrich interjected: "It is because of your daughter that I have lost my wife and child."

Jakob looked away, recognizing the man's deep pain. What could he say to someone so hurt? "I have lost my wife also; I know the pain," he said kindly. The magistrate's face softened. Jakob was surprised. But what was the greater surprise to Jakob was how his feelings for the magistrate changed at that moment. Despite all the offenses from the past, he felt a strong sense of love for the hard man standing before him. It was a love Jakob could not explain, and he wondered at it.

Jakob said, "I will pray for you to find solace." He immediately regretted his words as the magistrate's face hardened again.

"Do not pray for me; I will say my own prayers. I have much to do. Good day." He turned away from Jakob.

Arriving home, Jakob sat rubbing his eyes and feeling fatigued. He wrestled with the emotions he had felt at the meeting: anxiety, fear of failure, and then the love that had come so unexpectedly.

Mesmerized, Conrad watched Felix work. He sized up the printing press. At three feet wide and five or six feet long, it was longer than Felix was tall. Felix carefully took each letter from the pods he kept them in and painstakingly placed them in what he called the galley. When he had them all assembled, he put them in a frame, then placed the frame on a flat wooden plate.

"Would not it be better if that plate was metal?"

"So says the iron merchant's son." Felix looked up at Conrad with amusement.

"I'm just saying, it seems more practical."

"I'll think of replacing it with iron if that suits you," Felix said with a chuckle. He took out two wood pads mounted on handles and began to ink the type. When he had carefully covered the entire surface, he placed a piece of paper on top of it. Conrad watched him pull a big handle to bring down the top plate to press the type and paper. Afterward, Felix carefully removed the paper and they examined the image.

"I always marvel at this. I've done this work over and over, but this process of printing never ceases to amaze me when I look at the finished page."

Conrad stood staring at the paper. "What a difference this press has made to our work with the pamphlets and broadsides you print. The average person can then hear us read what we judge to be the truth." Conrad thought about the council and wondered what their response would be to Felix's latest broadside. "What is the name of this new one you are publishing?"

"It's called 'Protest and Defense.' I plan to present it to the council when we meet."

"What's the topic?" Conrad asked.

"I am defending our overall positions, especially why we don't want to baptize babies."

"What does it say?"

Felix pressed it into his chest forcefully. "Here. Read it for yourself."

Conrad began to read to himself.

"No, read it out loud!" Felix declared, standing with his hand on his chin.

"Should a man have the freedom to speak out in the public square? Should a man have the right to freedom of conscience? Does not God give us free will? And yet we do not have these rights to speak by our conscience here in this city. God has given us free will, but the city governors of Zurich suppress that very will. The governors restrain us. Judge for yourself. Is that right?"

Conrad handed the broadside back to Felix. "And you will read this to them?"

Felix answered, "Yes, if I'm allowed to."

"Will Zwingli be there, do you think?"

"Probably," Felix said in a disparaging tone.

"Good! I'd like to have a few words with him. There is something I've been considering lately. It is that no man is capable of stopping the truth. It lives, and it has a life of its own. That's our hope, isn't it? That the council sees that."

"I should be on my way," Conrad said. "Barbara will be watching for me. And you need to finish your printing." Conrad started for the door and nearly collided with William as he rushed into the press room. As he left, he heard William say, "Felix, I've got to talk to you!"

A knock came at Jakob's door. Felix stood outside, breathing heavily—something was amiss.

"What is it?" Jakob said. He showed Felix into the house and watched him collapse into a chair.

Felix breathed out heavily and said, "There is a rumor that I am intentionally stirring up the peasants, hoping they will go to war with the people of Zurich." He continued anxiously, "William came to the press to tell me this. It is the council spreading this lie."

Chapter 21

The Disputation

As Felix glanced around the council chamber, he was surprised to see only a handful in attendance. Jakob had not been invited, and Felix felt his absence. He would miss the comfort and support Jakob always gave. Jorg and Conrad were sitting in the back of the room. He took in their reassuring presence as they nodded toward him.

He glanced toward the door to see Huldrich Zwingli enter the room, carrying a ledger. Felix had expected him to attend and there he was. Felix became even more tense. *Zwingli*, he thought, *the man with the golden words, the one who so masterfully won the council last year in the debate with the Catholics over who had the right to rule the city.*

He swallowed hard. How would this meeting turn out? He shook his head and looked again at his friends. They had their heads together, talking and glancing at Zwingli.

"Felix Manz," the magistrate announced, startling Felix. Apprehension rocked him again.

"Yes, sir."

"You will now hear the accusations against you."

Felix listened to the list of familiar charges. There was nothing he did not expect until the exaggerations and falsehoods about war mongering and stirring up the peasants were read. He wondered why he was surprised. As the magistrate went on, Felix gripped the edge of the table with a force that mirrored the deep anger. His imaginings were taking him to places he shouldn't go. He felt himself holding his breath and began to pray. After a time, he could breathe again, but the anger still lodged within. He continued to grip the table, feeling that to be an outlet for the anger.

"Felix Manz, you will now answer these charges."

"I don't know how I would answer, with most of the charges being false or exaggerations," Felix said forcefully.

The chamber erupted, everyone talking at once.

The magistrate slammed his fist on the table. "Quiet! We will have order now! Manz, we will have you answer the charges."

Felix decided not to answer the charges directly. He was quiet for a time, attempting to get a grip on his emotions. He wished Jakob was there; that somehow, he would imbue Felix with his gentle, peacemaker spirit.

Felix held up his broadsides. "I have brought what I have printed," he said. "It explains our views."

"We will look at that later. Let's get on with this," the magistrate replied with disgust.

"I printed an explanation of our faith. I hoped you would respectfully look at it and take time to consider it." Felix looked defiantly at the magistrate and Zwingli.

Felix took a breath, and continued, "What the Brotherhood asks for is the freedom to follow our conscience. This council, not that long ago, asked for that same freedom. You dissented from the Catholics. At that time that brilliant debater," here he gestured toward Zwingli, who sat ramrod straight, not acknowledging what was said, "Zwingli, very capably, won the debate. Think of how it was when you were in our position. We appeal to your sense of justice. We ask that we might have the choices of free men, those who want to live by the dictates of the bible." He looked out over the room with a sense of hopelessness. He shook his head. "That's all I have to say, I have nothing more." He sat down with force.

It was the council's turn to speak. Felix, Jorg, Conrad, and a few others looked on as council members gave their opinions. It became obvious their minds had been made up long ago and they had only intended to give the impression that they were considering the matter.

The magistrate stood. "The council is in one accord. We will not change the city laws regarding baptism. You and your group must abide by them or there will be repercussions."

Felix jumped up, nearly knocking over his chair. "You demand freedom of religion for yourselves and then deny it to us."

Jorg stood and shouted from the back of the room, "I should not want a religion such as yours. We are like slaves, unable to make choices like free men."

"That is enough! Out with you all!" shouted the magistrate, standing and pointing toward the door.

As the three young men passed Zwingli on their way out, Conrad stopped and said, "What happened to you, Huldrich?" Zwingli's head jerked up. He appeared startled by Conrad's fury. "At one time you believed and taught the scripture. What happened to you?" Zwingli looked at the papers in his lap, choosing not to recognize his old friend. The three left, shaking their heads.

&

Later that evening, as they prepared for bed, Barbara swaddled her little one with protection on her mind. She said, "Conrad, did you expect anything other than how the meeting proved to be?"

"Jakob tried to warn us, didn't he? I knew the council was angry, but I was surprised at the level of emotion. It was chilling. In every encounter with them their level of outrage has grown. I wonder what is next? They make threats about coming repercussions, but they don't explain what they might be. It is very puzzling."

"I felt Felix was at the end of his patience," Barbara said, picking up Issabella and rocking her.

"It's hard to blame him. They accused him of purposely stirring up the peasants."

"No one likes to be lied about. They seem to especially target Felix," Barbara said.

"How are you feeling about all of this, Barbara?"

"I'm trying to make sense of it all. I feel unsettled and shaken. And I am afraid," she said, rocking the baby harder. "Those in power are trying to control us, to force us into their mold. What they insist on doesn't agree with the bible." She looked down at her little one and stroked her face. The baby smiled in response. Barbara said, "I'm so afraid for my Issabella, Conrad. Can they force us to baptize, although it goes against our beliefs?"

"We will *not* baptize our child. I promise you that!" Conrad cried. He sat quietly for a time. Then he said gently, "I remind you today, Barbara, as you have reminded me in the past." He looked lovingly into her eyes. "Don't give in to this fear. They want to control us with fear. Remember, scripture says over and over, 'Fear not!' So take courage, my love. God is our strength."

"Yes, I agree, we will trust Him with this." She took Conrad's hand. He grasped hers firmly and they pledged that they would trust in the Lord.

"You said that they have called another disputation?"

"Yes, it's to be at the old church, the Gross Muenster. The entire council is called to this one. They are expecting a large crowd. I hope Zwingli won't be there to debate."

"But you think he will?"

"Probably."

❧

Chapter 22

Heads down, shoulders slumped, and hearts weary, the three young men took a place at Jakob's table. Knowing the answer by their posture, Jakob nevertheless asked, "How did it go, lads?"

"Not well, sir. Not well at all," Felix answered. The others agreed, hands clasped in front of them, unwilling to look Jakob in the eye.

"Brothers, look at me." He waited. "Be strong. You have another opportunity; the next disputation is in two days. Consider how you can make amends. The Lord knows our situation and He knows it well."

Two peasants, one short and round, the other tall and thin and a bit emaciated, positioned themselves on the steps of the old church, observing the growing crowd.

"There he is, the one I told you about," the short man said. "Do you see him? The one with a head of white hair."

"That one?" The tall peasant pointed to Jakob.

"Yes, that's him. He's the master of the weavers guild. He had a cobbler make shoes for my family, children and all. We hadn't had proper shoes for a long time, and he gave us brand-new ones, he did. He is a great man, he is. Didn't have to do it—that's what my wife said. Shoes for the five little ones." He watched Jakob for a while. "He's a good man yes, he is."

"What do you think this meeting is about today?" the thin friend asked.

"Infant baptism, that's what it's about."

"I don't believe in it. We haven't baptized our last two little ones. No need. They can choose it later."

The two watched council members pass by them. The rotund friend spoke up: "Those are the great ones of the city."

"Great ones they may be but are they good ones? That's the question."

"There's Zwingli, the pastor of this great church. You have to admire him, don't you? His manner and the way he dresses." They stared at him as he passed. "We better get to our seats. It looks like the church might fill up. I don't know about you, but I don't want to miss the debate. It promises to be a good one."

The church *was* full. Conrad, Felix, and Jorg sat at a table in the front, facing the people. The council members filled up the front pews. City people sat behind them, and peasants filled the remaining space. In the very back sat the brethren—those with the courage to come, including Jakob, Priscilla, Barbara, and several others from their group. There was a great deal of noise, most of it from the peasants.

The magistrate strode to the front of the church, and faced the people. "People of Zurich! Quiet now!" he shouted. "This meeting is called to order." His voice echoed off the walls of the old church. Slowly, the people quieted.

"We meet today for a solemn event. We are here to decide between two points of view, just as we met that day to hear the dispute between the Roman church and Zwingli's reformed church. That debate was taken in an orderly, dignified manner, and I expect that to be the case today." He looked around the room with hawk-like, piercing eyes that rested on the peasants.

"First, we will hear from Felix Manz. Stand, Manz."

Felix stood, took a deep breath, and started, "My friends and I have been called today to deliver to you, Merciful Lords, an explanation of our beliefs. Some of you may know that we attempt to base our faith on the scripture, we look to the writings of those who have gone before. It is our desire to gain the wisdom of the old saints. A man in the second century by the name of Tertullian, a wise teacher of the faith, one who held common views with us of Christ and faith, said wise things."

Felix opened a book and read from it: "'It is a fundamental human right, a privilege of nature, that every man should worship according to his own convictions. It is assuredly no part of religion to compel religion—to which free will and not force, should lead us.'" Felix looked up from the book and continued. "Our consciences forbid us to baptize our babies. We do not see in scripture that Christ or the apostles instructed their followers to do this. It is clearly not in scripture. And yet this is what this council demands of us. The apostles taught and practiced as the meaning of baptism that only those who are transformed, who are taking on a new life, upon whom the spirit has come, and those convinced that they ought to be baptized. It must not be a ritual but an act of faith.

"So, I appeal to you, both for God's sake and the sake of the common name which we bear together. I want to bid you, wise Lords, to be willing to set aside personal interests, to analyze seriously, industriously, and fairly, the pure, clear truth as has been revealed to us through the scriptures and consider well what we deal with here." Felix sat, exhausted.

The magistrate moved to the front of the church, saying, "Now we will turn the debate over to the honorable pastor of this church, Huldrich Zwingli."

All eyes were on Zwingli as he rose with great pomp and moved toward the podium. He stood for a moment gazing over those gathered. Casting a glance toward the young men, he said, "We have three men on trial this day. Conrad Grebel, known to his family as a disgrace for many years." Conrad turned his head away. "Jorg Blaurock, the representative Catholic." Here he emphasized *Catholic*. "And Felix Manz. We all know of your reputation, don't we?" he began.

❧

"Tomorrow we will know our fate . . . finally," Conrad told his friends as they sat at Jakob's table.

Barbara studied his face, trying to determine his mood. She said, "I thought Felix did a masterful job conveying our views, don't you think so, Conrad?"

"Yes . . . but for Zwingli. He's a brilliant debater and he has proved it again, hasn't he?"

Barbara nodded, keeping her eyes on her husband, "He has indeed."

"As I listened, it felt as if Zwingli tore down our entire tower of belief, stone by stone, and there it sat in a lonely pile in the middle of the room."

With his big hand, Jakob covered Conrad's trembling one. "You know that is not true, brother. Our views stand as truth and will not be shaken."

"I know. But that's how it felt at the time." Conrad said, discouragement covering his face. "Tomorrow the verdict will be posted."

❧

The next day, Priscilla and Jakob slowly walked to the square. They came to see for themselves if what people were saying was true.

Priscilla read the first poster that had been nailed up earlier in the day. "This one says you, father, are no longer a member of the council."

"Well, that's no surprise. I was expecting it."

Reading the next post, Jakob said with a loud sigh, "This one I didn't expect."

"What does it say?"

"It says we can no longer meet for bible study. They have made it illegal."

Priscilla gasped. They stared at the poster in disbelief.

"What does the last one say, daughter? I dread it."

Priscilla gasped again, staring at the poster, fear on her face. "It's true what the others have said."

"What is it?" Jakob moved closer to read for himself. "Proclamation of the Council of the city of Zurich, on this January 18, the year of our Lord 1525, those of the city who refuse to baptize their children will have eight days to comply or risk banishment."

Jakob shook his head. "Now we know." It was true. A great change was coming.

Chapter 23

Lord, grant to me a quiet mind

Priscilla sat reflecting on the previous day's events. The questions had rested between them for a time. What would the future bring? Would the council make good on its threats? Now she and Jakob knew the answer. But with that came another question: If the council was willing to demand that families of the brethren with babies leave the city, did that mean they would come for the families of those without babies? Would they find a reason to come for the rest of them? As Priscilla thought about these things, emotions hit her in a powerful way, and she teetered between anger and fear. She was certain Felix would not give up his street preaching, which presented a danger for all of them. What if the council chose to banish *all* the brethren because of their association with him?

She sat fully dressed in front of the small fireplace in her bedroom, wrapped in a blanket. It had been an especially cold night. The fire struggled and so did she. Her imagination went wild with the possibilities. What if they had to leave everything? She thought about all the things she loved about her home: the tapestries on the walls, the furniture that had been in her family for generations, the big wooden door with its beautiful carvings. She had always thought of the door as a protector. Would it protect them now? Other things she loved, like her garden, resting now but ready to come alive in the spring. Would she be asked to give these things up for her faith? How could she? She felt as if she were being torn apart, and her life, as Conrad had said, seemed to lie like broken shards on the floor. The emotion was like pain to her. She couldn't give all this up . . . could she?

Taking a deep breath, Priscilla sat for a time in the stillness of the room. A scripture came to her as she meditated on what was happening in her heart: *Love not the world nor the things of the world.* She put her hand over her mouth; it felt as if her heart had stopped. She said aloud, "Yes, yes, that's it? What have I been thinking? I have been so caught up in my fears."

During the morning stillness, she thought about how that scripture had called her to itself. *Love not the world.* If she were to listen, she felt certain she would have peace. She prayed to be set free and began to repent her selfish thoughts, her fears, and her love of possessions. Again, she sat quietly, meditating more. Then something unexpected happened. She paused. *There it was, that sound. Had she felt it or heard it?* It was like ice breaking. A sound she had heard before, when stepping on small frozen puddles in the street as she walked through the city. But this—this was the sound of her heart, breaking free.

After more prayer and thanksgiving, she felt drawn to her desk. She sat at it and looked over her poems. She remembered a line she had written months earlier, but she hadn't been sure where it would fit: *O, fret not thyself.* She stayed with that for a moment, rolling the line around in her head. Then, more came: *Far in the future lieth a fear, like a long, low mist of grey, gathering to fall in dreary rain, thus doth thy heart within thee complain.* What if she somehow added to that to: *O fret not thyself, nor let thy heart be troubled, neither let it be afraid.*

She gasped. It was happening, her poetry was opening up, coming alive! She sat back in her chair and rejoiced at the thought. She ran the words over and over in her mind, becoming more excited about the possibilities of this poem. She stared into the flame of the candle on her desk, not certain how the poem would fit together and fill out. She was grateful to God. She felt that it must have been her repentance and how it had changed her heart. Another stanza came to her, and she wrote it down. She felt she must share this. "I've got to talk to Barbara," she said aloud. Wrapped against the cold, she started off for the home of her friend.

Arriving, she knocked hard at the door. When no one answered, she walked in to see Conrad and Felix, their eyes wide, staring at her.

"Priscilla, it's you!" Conrad said with relief. She realized they were on high alert. Had they imagined she was Heinrich, the magistrate, here to arrest them?

"Yes, just me. May I speak with Barbara?"

"She is getting the baby from the other room," Conrad answered.

"I'll wait here." She sat down. *How weary they looked.* "How do you two feel after the events of late?"

Felix said, "I have not slept well lately, I've been writing without stop since the disputation."

"I haven't slept well either," said Conrad, "but somehow I feel energized."

She saw the encouragement on his face and breathed a sigh of relief.

In walked Barbara with the baby.

Priscilla said, "Please, may I hold her?" Taking the baby in her arms, she said, "She is growing so fast, and she's so beautiful. What is she now, two weeks old?"

The two men continued their conversation and Barbara and Priscilla moved to a corner to talk. Barbara sat with the baby in her lap waiting.

"Barbara, my poetry is back," Priscilla said excitedly, no longer able to hold it in.

Barbara looked at her with admiration. "I'm so happy for you, my friend."

Holding a small book she used for writing, Priscilla asked, "Could I read some of it to you?"

"Please do." Barbara leaned in to listen as Priscilla read the poem she had worked on earlier.

Afterward, Barbara said with awe, "That's so beautiful Priscilla. It's true, isn't it? Your gift is back."

Priscilla smiled. "It's not complete, but I am seeing progress. Let me tell you what happened earlier today."

Chapter 24

The Prayer Meeting
I have seen a fiery flame

Priscilla and her father put on their cloaks, preparing to leave. "We don't know what to expect of this meeting, do we father?"

"No, we don't. It has been a season of the unexpected." Jakob opened the door and they made their way through the dark city to meet with the others.

"Our hope is that those who watch us these days won't suspect our meeting at Felix's mother's home. It's nicely tucked in a sort of out-of-the-way part of the city," Priscilla commented as they hurried on, keeping an eye open for those who might be watching their movements.

They arrived at their destination and chatted a bit with friends. Then Jakob started the meeting by opening his bible.

He began to read a part of scripture that had spoken to them in the past. He read, "Dear friends, do not be surprised at the painful trial you are suffering, as though something strange were happening to you. But rejoice that you participate in the sufferings of Christ.'" He looked up at the three young men, then continued, "'So that you be overjoyed when His glory is revealed.'" He closed his bible, extended his arm toward them, and said, "I turn the meeting into the capable hands of the young preachers."

Conrad, Felix, and Jorg walked to the front of the room. Jorg addressed the group solemnly. "We all know our great need during this time, and we know we must go to our Source. Therefore, we have called that this time be dedicated to calling out to our great master, Jesus." They went to their knees as they had done many times and called out to the Lord to help them to do His divine will, asking for His mercy.

When they finished praying, Jorg stood up, turned to Conrad, and said, "I have not been baptized as an adult, and I feel convicted that I should take that step now. Will you baptize me, brother?" Jorg knelt again, and as the others watched, tears formed and ran down his face. Conrad placed his hands on Jorg's shoulders and began to pray while one of the young women ran to the kitchen area to get a pitcher of water. Conrad baptized Jorg in the name of the Father, Son, and the Holy Spirit. Then, to their surprise, a divine quiet fell over them. Experiencing this, the others in the group turned to Jorg and asked if he would baptize them. One by one, those who had not been baptized took their turn.

The last one was Felix's mother. Felix watched as his little mother walked toward him. She looked up at her tall son and said, "Will you baptize me?"

"I will, Mother." He took the pitcher of water from Jorg. She sat in the chair, and as Priscilla cradled her head with a towel, Felix baptized her. She stood and with tears running down her face, leaned on her son, laying her head on his chest. He put his arms around her. "Thank you for loving me and caring for me despite your many trials in life," he said. "I know it has not been easy for you." Felix spoke a few more words over her, kissed her cheek, and they faced the others. Once again, a holy glory and stillness fell over the room.

Some stood. Others knelt. All bowed their heads, feeling suspended in that powerful moment. Nothing was said for a time. No one wanted to break the peace. Then it was over, as suddenly as it had come. They looked at each other as if to say, *What just happened?*

Then the laughter and joy came. It was like a refreshing rain, and it carried their sorrows away. They were changed. From that time on, when they talked of that night, they would tell how they felt a boldness from the Lord and the inner strength to go on, when before they had been certain they could not.

❧

Chapter 25

Priscilla and her father sat at the table breaking their morning fast with fresh bread and goat milk. She was watching him. He glanced at her, knowing what she was thinking. "The young men are calling it the beginning of the free church," he said. "I like the sound of that, the free church."

"Yes, they have new energy, a holy boldness, don't they? Papa, have you ever experienced anything like that, the prayer meeting, I mean? The way we felt that night?"

"No, I have not. It was a rare atmosphere. A certain awe and amazement came to us. The presence of the Lord was there in a mighty way. A unity came, like a blanket we took and wrapped around ourselves. No, I have never experienced anything like it. Maybe I never will again. I cherish that time."

They sat in silence for a moment.

"Oh, I meant to tell you," Priscilla said, "I had planned to barter with our neighbor Marguerite for root vegetables this year. Remember how I told you our crop came out poorly?"

"Yes, I do."

"I'm having second thoughts now."

"Why?"

"From conversations with her, I know she sides with the council. She has been harsh and judgmental in the past. I'm not sure of her attitude toward us now. There is such anger all around, she may have changed her mind about the barter. Many people have turned against us. The council has made sure of it."

"We can't change this, but you made an agreement with our neighbor and should make good on it. She will have herbs and we will have the vegetables we need for the rest of the winter."

Priscilla sighed. "Yes, you're right. I need to make good on it." She was thankful for his wisdom.

Priscilla walked toward Marguerite's house wondering what she might face. At the door she swallowed and knocked. Marguerite ushered her in. She was still willing to make the barter, but treated Priscilla coldly, wearing a scowl the entire time. After they exchanged goods, she dismissed Priscilla with a prickly wave of her hand. The sting of that exchange rested on Priscilla as she looked at the heavy bags on the ground before her. *How would she get them home?* Just then, she heard someone say, "Need some help?"

She looked up surprised to see William sitting before her in his cart. "Yes, thank you," she said.

He jumped down and loaded the cart. As Priscilla climbed into it, she said, "I guess I have overprepared with the number of vegetables I've bartered for. Or perhaps I should say, under-prepared. I don't know how I ever thought I would be able to carry this amount," she added with a little chuckle, feeling encouraged by William's presence.

Nothing more was said between them until they reached Priscilla's house. Then William spoke. "They're watching you."

"What?"

"Some of the council members. They're still watching your group and your movements. They plan to keep watch over you and your activities," he whispered, leaning close to her.

She caught her breath, unaccustomed to the closeness of a man. After a moment to right herself, she said, "We thought as much. We have begun to meet at different homes where we have not previously met." She looked at William and thought, *I don't really know him, do I?* "What about you, William? Doesn't meeting with us endanger your position with the council?"

"I don't care," he said with determination, looking straight ahead. "I don't care what they think." She saw the resolution in his face and remembered how he had joined them when they walked out on the first disputation.

"I have come to believe as you and your father do," he said, turning to her. "I see your lives and the lives of the others, and I believe now." William sat pensively, holding the reins. The horse whined as she waited for William to go on. "Priscilla, I wanted to tell you about what has happened to me recently." He looked straight ahead again. *How interesting,* she thought, having just considered how little she knew him.

"Several nights ago, I left a council meeting where they were again criticizing your group. It seems the only order of business lately. I reached my home feeling burdened, and as I walked around looking at all the possessions I own, I thought about how I had lived in this big house by myself all these years. I began to feel alone and empty. What does this mean to me, I thought? I sat that night with a sense of emptiness, and I began to pray, as I had never prayed before. Then something happened to me I can't explain. It was as if the Holy Spirit gripped me. I started the night empty and ended it filled with joy."

"When did this happen, William?"

"Two nights ago," he said.

"William, that was the very time of the prayer meeting," Priscilla said with wonder. "You probably didn't know this, we met at Felix's mother's house to pray together, and Jorg ended up baptizing people. There was a great stirring and, yes, it was as if we were gripped and filled with the Holy Spirit. And just as you said, we had never experienced anything like it."

Their eyes met for a moment, and she saw something different there. Something softer, gentler, yet intense. It drew her in a way she didn't understand.

"I don't feel alone now. Not after that experience . . . and with you here," William said softly, looking at her with gentle eyes. This unexpected admission made Priscilla uncomfortable.

Hoping to change the subject, she said, "What will you do about this, William?"

"I don't know yet. Perhaps in the future, I will be banned from the council as your father has been. But as I said, it no longer matters to me."

"You should talk to my father, William. He will have some wisdom for you."

Chapter 26

Jakob sat on a chair at the back of the guild hall instructing a new apprentice in the art of linen weaving. He was interrupted by a voice from behind him.

"Are you busy, Jakob? I can come back later if need be."

Jakob turned to see Josef, the plowman and preacher he had met at the guild hall several weeks earlier. "No, my friend. Of course, we must talk, and you have come a long distance. Follow me to the back." On the way, Jakob stopped to talk to some of the newer members of the guild, adding some encouragement.

Then they settled into chairs around a small table. After some pleasantries, Josef said solemnly, "We have heard about the disputation and the council decision. How is the community doing?"

Jakob answered, "It was quite unsettling. I suppose we should have seen it coming. But, of course, we hoped against hope." He smiled at Josef. "But I must say it has caused us to grow closer together as a group. We feel now that we are alienated from the others in the city; we have only each other. We have been driven to prayer as never before. And we have had a time of prayer as we've never experienced before. We feel changed, Josef. God is taking something that appeared on the outside to be perilous, and He is turning it into a blessing."

Josef nodded. "This is how it often goes, isn't it?

They sat sharing common experiences and a bond grew between them.

When it was time to leave Josef said, "Let us take a time of prayer." With their heads close together they went humbly to the Lord. After prayer, Josef had one more thing to share. "Before I go, I wanted to say that you might be interested in meeting a man in Waldshut, just north of Zurich. Do you know Waldshut?"

"Yes, I've been there."

"I believe I have mentioned him before. His name is Balthasar Hubmaier. I'm sure you and he would find much agreement. I would like to invite you to visit our town. Perhaps in the future it may be needed as a place of refuge." Josef looked on with concern.

"While we don't know what the future will hold, we well know this," Josef said. "I have a cabin where you and your daughter could stay while you visit. It's not as fine as your present home, I'm sure, but perhaps when the weather clears and you feel you could travel, you might come to our town. Things are different in Waldshut. An army of peasants guards us against those who oppose our convictions."

"That is a generous offer, friend. I feel we will take you up on it," Jakob said, nodding. "You surely aren't traveling to Waldshut today?"

"No, I am staying with friends outside the city. There are many outside the city walls that yearn to hear the word of God, and it's my job to bring it to them. I don't tread far these days but come nicer weather I will take up my route again," Josef said in his congenial way.

As the two said their goodbyes, Josef had one last thing to add: "I was wondering, Jakob, would you have an extra loom or two for some of the peasants to use? They gather in a large room in Waldshut, praying and working together. It would be a great blessing to them. Life is hard for the peasants, especially lately. They continue to suffer. If you could help in any way, it would be appreciated." Planning to meet another time, Jakob walked Josef outside to his cart and horse and watched Josef head down the street.

Later that day, as Jakob walked the cobblestone street, he mulled over this meeting. In his mind's eye, he could see Josef's hands, big and calloused, the hands of a man of the earth, one who worked the land that was so unwilling some years. It was a fight and hard work, and it took determination. Josef struggled with the land and with those who opposed his beliefs. Some called these preachers the plowmen. Jakob called them strong and courageous. He was determined to help Josef's people.

Chapter 27

Leaving for the guild that morning, Priscilla watched sadly as two families from the Brotherhood drove down the street, obviously preparing to leave the city with their carts packed and overflowing with their goods. It was becoming an everyday experience. One family had children in the back of their cart. The mother sat in the front, holding twins, one of them crying. They stopped to say goodbye to her.

"We're not going to give them the satisfaction of banishing us," the mother said, looking at her children with apprehension. Turning to Priscilla, she added, "Goodbye, dear sister."

"Goodbye, and may God bless you," Priscilla said with a heavy heart.

Priscilla continued to the guild, thinking about how the exodus had slowed the work there as weavers left. There was also Jakob's gentle, but ongoing appeal to hear, and if they were willing, and to respond to the message of the gospel. Each day, he spoke of the Lord and His command to love one another. Jakob never compelled any of them, just taught them to love, and he loved them individually. With that, they saw Jesus.

The brethren now had to be careful when they met. Some council members had begun stopping into the guild unannounced. She marveled at how her father always seemed to know when they were coming. She smiled to herself and walked on.

❧

Jakob sat in his chair taking questions from his weavers that morning as he mulled over the council becoming more vigilant with their rules and regulations in their attempt to stop the group. He frowned. What if the guild was taken from him? What if he was forced out of the city? His head journeyman, Michael, was very capable and could take over the work. This gave Jakob some consolation. What's more, he thought about how he was getting older and wouldn't be around forever.

Jakob watched Priscilla work at her loom. At that moment, William strode through the door. Jakob thought about the changes he had seen in William lately. He was a fine man and had been a good friend to their group.

After a brief chat with Jakob, William excused himself to greet Priscilla.

"I haven't seen you at the loom before," William told her.

"Well, now you have," she said, stopping the loom. "I help when needed. Let me show you the work my father and I relish the most, what we are working on now."

They approached a tapestry hung on a vertical loom at the back of the large room. Surveying the work together they stood very close—so close that Priscilla felt William's warmth. It made her a little uncomfortable, but she didn't move. She hadn't felt a man's warmth next to her in a long while. Glancing up at William, she saw he was intently examining the piece and she felt proud.

"I have seen a similar piece at one of the noble's homes, but this one is exquisite. And part of it is your work?"

"I designed it and I have done most of the handwork. There were problems with these two trees." She pointed them out. "I wanted them to look as if they were moving slightly but couldn't capture what I saw in my mind's eye. My father took that on. And I think he accomplished it." She tilted her head to look at the piece again. "It's very close now to what I imagined."

"What was your inspiration for this beautiful design?"

"I keep my eyes open, not wanting to let spark or vision escape my imagination," she said playfully.

With his eyes still on the piece, William nodded. He surprised Priscilla with, "I plan to be at the meeting tonight."

"Good. We gather at seven."

William smiled at her, excused himself, and was on his way out the door.

When she was seated at her loom again, her father stood near her for a time and watched her work. After a few moments, he said, "I have observed William often seeks you out for conversation, daughter."

With her head down, she didn't notice the sparkle in her father's eyes. "What do you mean? Why do you comment on William? I thought he came to speak to you," she said, absorbed in her weaving.

"He appears to have a special interest in you, Priscilla."

She looked up at her father with a knitted brow. "I believe you have an overactive imagination, Papa."

"And I believe you need to open your eyes to the obvious," Jakob said with a small smile.

She shook her head, glanced at the door William had exited through, and returned to her work.

❧

Chapter 28

Jakob admired Remy's tools hanging on the wall, every tool a cobbler would need: awls, knives, and needles. Just then, he turned toward the door to see Remy burst into the room. "Want to watch me work, Master Jakob?"

"I would, indeed."

Remy moved toward a bowl of water on the table and picked a piece of leather out of it. "First," he said, "I soak the leather in warm water. That makes it easy to work with. This has been soaking for a time."

"How long do you soak the leather?" Jakob asked.

"Until it feels right to me. Some pieces are thicker or just different. This piece feels ready. I'll take it out and dry it a bit. Then I take my knife and begin to cut the top part of the shoe in this pattern. Can you see how this will wrap around the foot? Do you see it?" Remy looked to Jakob for affirmation.

"And what kind of leather is this piece?" Jakob asked, touching it briefly.

"This is the top of the shoe and it's goat skin."

Jakob watched as Remy skillfully used the knife to cut the piece. He marveled at the speed at which Remy worked.

"There. Now I'll work with what will be the sole of the shoe. This leather is cowhide. It's thicker and stronger. It has been soaked also. Now I'll cut some leather laces."

Remy sewed the two pieces together then turned them inside out, so the seam was concealed. "After it dries completely, I apply beeswax to soften and season the leather. Later, I'll cut holes with the awl on the top and put in the leather laces. Then I'm done. I'll hang them with the others on the rope on the other side of the room. Then I can move on to the next one. That's the process."

"Do you enjoy the work, Remy?"

"I do. I like the smell of the leather. Not everyone does, but I do, and I like working with the wax. I'd prefer to sit outside in the sun to work. Soon it will be warmer and it will be comfortable working there. Yes, it feels good to be at it again, to be useful."

"Remy, I was wondering, what do you think about opening up your business here to others? Selling to the wider public, not just working for me?"

"Do you mean in addition to helping the peasants with shoes?" Remy's eyes shone.

"Yes, that's what I was thinking," Jakob said. "I would still want a number of shoes, but you should have your own interests also. What do you think?"

Remy paused to consider the proposal. He said excitedly, "I suppose I would have to start slowly and build from there. But that sounds good."

"I would, of course, continue to pay you for what you produce for the peasants, does that sound like a deal?"

"I am most grateful for the opportunity, Master Jakob," Remy said with a slight bow.

"You've worked very hard here, and I'm thankful for your service. I'll need to get on to the work of the guild now. It never ends!" Jakob said with a chuckle. "Oh Remy," he said, "I want to invite you to the meeting tonight. We must be careful these days when we meet because of the council but we are still at it."

"Yes, the council." Remy thought of how his friends Conrad and Jorg had had to leave Zurich so quickly to protect the new baby and because they no longer felt safe in the city.

"We are meeting at Katrina and her husband's home tonight. Do you know where it is? We can no longer meet here at the guild or at my home, it's too dangerous. Will you be able to join us?"

Perhaps Anna will be there, Remy thought, and answered quickly, "Yes, I will."

❧

Remy walked the quiet, dark streets toward Katrina's. He was glad the moon was out because he was unsure which house belonged to Katrina and her husband, and now he wasn't certain he was on the right street. Then he saw it. The curtains were drawn; it looked like no one was home. He knocked and waited. The door opened a crack and Katrina's husband Michael peeked out. "Remy! Welcome, come in." He grabbed Remy's arm and pulled him in. "We must be ever so careful you know. You've heard of the council and their abuse toward us?"

"Of course," Remy said, standing warily just inside the door.

"It's just you haven't been to the meetings lately, I wasn't sure you knew. Come in, come in. Good to see you."

Despite the ongoing hostility the brethren faced, there was an atmosphere of joy and celebration in the room and Remy felt it. He took up his usual spot near a wall and began to search the group for Anna. Would she talk to him tonight? He spotted her as she walked in from the other room and began serving food to others as they stood chatting. He thought she looked especially beautiful tonight.

Jakob walked up to Remy and stopped in front of him, unintentionally obscuring his view. "I'm glad you've come, Remy," he said. "It's probably good to be among friends, I was thinking of you all alone in that big house of Conrad's."

"Yes, it can be lonely," Remy replied, glimpsing Anna walking into the kitchen.

"Remy, do you ever see people watching Conrad's house?"

"Yes, it's very irritating," Remy said, his eyes on the door Anna had disappeared through. "I chased one off yesterday."

"Others of the community are being watched. You chased him away." Jakob patted Remy on the back. "Well then, I admire your bravery, Remy," Jakob said.

"Good evening, Jakob."

Remy turned to see Anna standing next to him addressing Jakob. She turned toward him and said, "Hello Remy. We haven't seen you for a while."

There it was for Remy, the awkwardness again. He wondered why she had this effect on him. He scrambled to keep her attention.

"I've been busy at the guild hall cobbling. Master Jakob has me employed, you know."

"He says your skills are very useful and helpful to the peasants," Anna said in her sweet, delicate way, causing Remy to admire her even more.

Hoping desperately to impress her, he said, "And I'm going to be a more permanent resident in the city. I will be setting up my own business cobbling as well."

She smiled at him and said, "How very nice." His heart sped up as he looked at her, but again, he had no idea what to say.

She solved his problem. "I must be off now," she said. "I'm serving tonight, helping Katrina. She has a new baby, you know."

Words now came to Remy. He said hurriedly," I was wondering, Anna, maybe we can talk later." She nodded with a reserved look.

When the meeting ended, Remy approached Anna again. "It's such a nice evening, warm and everything. What about a walk?"

"Some of us walk down to the river after the meetings. You could join us." Remy was disappointed to have to share Anna with others. Gazing at her, he thought, *She seems so alive and more beautiful than ever. I want to kiss her.*

She interrupted his thoughts. "It's very peaceful at the river. Do you want to join us? We usually stop on the bridge."

There were six of them walking that night, feeling the lovely freedom of the evening and the joy of being together. The heaviness of the last few weeks was forgotten. They were just young people without a care.

Remy and Anna walked at the back of the group. They talked about their shared experiences of missing Conrad, Barbara, the baby, and Jorg. Remy flirted with Anna, entertaining her with stories of Jorg and his antics. He told her about how they met in the woods and stayed in barns outside the city when it got colder. Anna told him how she watched Jorg preach and how the people loved him.

"I miss them also," she said. "It must have been difficult sleeping out in the cold, but then Conrad invited you to stay with him."

"That allowed me to meet you, Anna," Remy said with affection. He thought he saw Anna respond. With that exchange on each of their hearts, they continued walking down the street enjoying the quiet of the night. Remy slowed his pace so that eventually the rest of the group was out of sight. He wanted to be alone with Anna. He had wanted this for a long time and now it was happening—he had her all to himself.

Finally, they reached the bridge. They stood close, their arms touching, and they watched the river flow to Lake Zurich.

Anna looked up at the high twin towers of the old church, the Gross Muenster, towering over them. She said, "Felix told us one night when we walked this way that the man who was once the head canon of this church was his father."

"It was a joke among the peasants: the priests and their 'wives'," Remy said sarcastically.

Anna looked away, hurt on her face. "It was a very painful thing for Felix. Many in the city criticized him and his mother." She stared at the towers saying, "Priscilla says that's why he's especially singled out by the council, because of his association with the Catholics and his birth circumstances. That's why they are so hateful toward him."

Remy eyed the river. He said nothing, thinking about injustices.

"We should catch up with the group. What if bandits are out tonight?" Anna said fearfully.

"You are with Remy," he said, his swagger returning. "There is nothing to fear." He took her hand, looked deeply into her eyes, and, kissing her hand, he said, "It's getting late. We can walk toward your house."

As they walked down the cobblestone street, Remy put his arm around her shoulder. He realized this was his chance. He began to tell her how much he cared for her.

Finally, she said, "There's something I have to tell you." Remy saw the pleading in her eyes. "My story is like Felix's." Starting at the beginning, she told him her story.

"You're with child by that priest!" A deep desire to protect her arose in him and it could be felt in the atmosphere as they walked. "He misused you, Anna. Remy was quiet for a time, thinking the matter over. "Don't you hate him for it?"

He stopped walking to look at her and was confused by the sadness on her face.

"No, I don't hate him. That's my problem, I should hate him, but I don't."

"Well, I hate him for it. How he's treated you and what he's done," Remy said with intensity. He saw something stir in Anna. "Let's stop here." He put his arms around her waist, pulled her close to him, and felt her melt into him. Bringing his head close to hers, he brushed her lips with his. When she didn't object, he placed his lips upon her warm ones and kissed her as he had never kissed a woman. He took his lips away and watched as she slowly opened her eyes.

"You kiss me like that even though you have heard my story?" she said with wonder.

"I told you how much I care for you," he whispered in her ear as he held her.

"We should go, Priscilla is probably waiting for me," Anna said. They moved on, walking slowly, not talking, an awkwardness settling between them. When they arrived at her door, Anna said, "Thank you for keeping me safe, Remy."

Before he could respond, she opened the door and was gone, leaving him looking after her, wondering what had happened. The night wasn't supposed to end like this. What had he done wrong?

❧

Chapter 29

"Anna, are you all right? You are out very late, and I worried about bandits detaining you—or worse." Priscilla wore a troubled look as she held the door open.

"I wasn't alone. Some of the brethren walked by the river and Remy joined us."

"Remy joined. I'm surprised."

"As was I," Anna said, her head down. Priscilla sat down in the chair across from her, wondering at Anna's dark mood.

"The evening was wonderful. Remy was so sweet and tender to me. He told me stories about Jorg and their adventures together before we met them. We laughed and had such fun. He was gentle, and kind, and he held my hand." Anna glanced up at Priscilla. "I didn't know he was that sort of man. I've never been treated like that, Priscilla, with that kind of affection. Never." She paused. "I told him my entire story . . . even the baby."

"Oh, child. What was his response?"

"He was enraged at Fredrik . . . and then he said something . . . I don't know what to think about it." She looked up at Priscilla. "He told me he loved me. And that he had loved me from the first time he saw me."

"What?"

"After what life has dealt me, I didn't think a decent man would want me."

"It looks like Remy wants you, Anna."

"I don't know what to think, Priscilla. I'm confused. And I'm afraid."

A little later, Jakob, Priscilla, and Anna sat before the fire. Father and daughter talked about the last meeting, the latest threats from the council, and how those threats were setting their friends on edge. Anna looked into the fire, pensive and troubled. Priscilla sighed, unsure how to comfort Anna, when a knock came at the door. Priscilla and Jakob looked at each other. *Who would be at the door at this hour?*

Jakob opened the door and there stood Conrad. "Conrad! What a surprise." Poking his head out the door, looking up and down the street, he whispered, "Is this safe for you to be here?"

"Are you going to let me in?" Conrad said with a slight smile.

"Of course, I was just so surprised." Jakob laughed at himself. "Come in. Warm yourself at the fire and sit in my chair right here."

Conrad was greeted wholeheartedly and quickly sat down. "I was preaching near the city, and I became a little homesick for my friends," Conrad said, looking at the three of them with affection. And this house. We have had so many sweet times of fellowship here." He smiled at his friends. "I've been anxious to tell you what's been happening this spring with our preaching to those outside the city, where we have ministered lately.

"Many are coming to the Lord, and it's miraculous, really. Since Jorg and I set up to preach in a small town we are amazed at the response of peasants. We are seeing many more coming and committing to God. The people are hungry for the Lord, wanting to hear the word of God. And we see those who are hard and bitter about the peasant wars and their treatment by the landowners. They fall on their knees and repent with tears. The plowman, those big men with their weathered faces, tears rolling down them. It's something I've never seen before, the fruit of prayers I'm certain."

"So God took something that looked bad to us and is bringing good from it. You having to leave the city, I mean," Priscilla said, repeating something she had heard her father say many times.

"Yes, I wonder at that myself. But we had to leave, Priscilla. I promised Barbara we wouldn't be subject to the council and their laws about baptism. And Jorg and I thought we were a threat to the safety of the brethren. We had to go. How are things here in Zurich after the prayer meeting?"

"We are forever changed, that's certain," Jakob replied. "But if you mean the council, they continue in their threats toward us. We still manage to meet for bible studies, but we must stay hidden again. We move from house to house. We no longer meet at the guild."

"Many have left the city with their babies," Priscilla added.

"Where is Barbara, is she safe?" Anna interjected.

"She stays with friends."

"And Issabella?"

"She's growing fast. And what about you, Anna? You will have a little one soon and what will you do?"

Jakob interrupted, "We were thinking about visiting Waldshut to determine if it would be a safe place for Anna and possibly, in the future, for Priscilla and me, if need be. Have you heard what's happening there?"

"No, tell me," Conrad said.

"Balthasar Hubmaier has taken control of the city council. As a result, there is freedom for the people to worship as they please. Also, a peasant army surrounds the city and protects their freedoms."

Hearing this, Conrad sat upright. "How amazing. Let's pray that this movement will spread to the other areas."

"Perhaps your preaching will open more hearts and we will see this," Jakob added.

"It's getting late, and I will have to leave in a few hours. May I rest here until then?"

Jakob nodded. "You can, of course. Our house is always open to you, old friend."

Jumping up, Priscilla said, "Let me gather some food for you to take. I have some salted meat and bread baked just this morning."

The two men talked on, unwilling to say goodbye. "Our lives have been so closely intertwined this last year and now I don't know if I will see you again, Jakob."

"That's one of the crosses we must bear, isn't it?" Jakob said.

Later, standing at the door, Conrad said, "Jakob, you have been my teacher and like a father to me."

"Where will you go, Conrad?"

"Back to where I left Jorg. We will continue in our mission."

They embraced and Conrad was gone.

Jakob left early the next morning for the guild, whistling as he walked down the street, his mood bolstered by the evening with Conrad. Still whistling he walked into the building. Michael, the head journeyman, who stood over the work of one of the apprentices said, "Good morning, Master Jakob, some good news for you?" He was aware of his master's burdens.

At that moment, the magistrate burst through the door and scanned the room. Seeing Jakob, he marched toward him and said, "I will see you now in the back of the guild."

Jakob followed him.

Whipping around, the magistrate faced Jakob and said, "Conrad Grebel was seen at your home last night." With a fierce look, the magistrate continued, "Let me remind you, Jakob, you are not to have bible studies here or at any other place. And I recommend that you don't harbor people who are a threat to our authority. Do you understand?" Jakob said nothing. "Do you understand?" the magistrate said loudly.

"I hear what you say, yes, but I must follow my conscience."

Heinrich stared at him for a time, shook his head in disgust, and stomped out of the room. Turning as he reached the front door he said, "You could lose more than you can imagine."

Jakob let out the breath he had been holding and relaxed his shoulders. He knew what he must do. "Michael," he said, "could you watch over the guild this coming week? I have some business to attend to."

"Of course, Master Jakob, if that's what you need."

Jakob nodded and left the building.

❧

Chapter 30

"Tomorrow we leave for Waldshut," Jakob said. "I'll pick up the cart and horse tonight. Pack up all of Anna's belongings. We will stop and ask Josef if the cabin he offered us is still available." Jakob looked affectionately at Anna. "Anna will stay there, and she will be safe."

"What about you and me?" Priscilla said, apprehensively.

"After what the magistrate said, I'm not sure any of us are safe here anymore," Jakob replied with a sigh.

"Papa, what are you saying?"

"I don't know what the magistrate meant when he said we might lose what we have, Priscilla. I believe the council is capable of that which we cannot and do not want to imagine. We are taking precautions. Perhaps, as Josef said, Waldshut is a place of refuge for us. We must look at our options and make our plans."

Priscilla knelt by her bed that night, as always, but her prayer was different. "Oh God, be our protector, be our Hightower, and let us be hidden in you."

Ȣ

The next morning, they prepared for the journey that would take most of the day. They packed the cart with Anna's few precious things: her books, clothes, and keepsakes her parents had given her.

"Are you comfortable there, Anna?" Priscilla turned to look at Anna sitting in the cart. Then she turned back toward her father. "She wouldn't complain if she wasn't comfortable, would she, Papa?"

He shook his head, looked at Anna, and smiled. They sat for a few minutes in front of the house, unwilling to leave. As they waited, Priscilla looked at the large ornate wooden door, remembering the day it was set in place. She and Jakob had been so proud of it. It seemed to protect them against the outside world; she no longer knew if that were true.

Jakob took the reins and guided the horse into the street. Priscilla watched as the streets took her away from her home. They rounded a corner. She couldn't see the house now, and they headed out of the city.

Hoping to lighten their heavy hearts, Priscilla said, "I'm looking forward to the trip through the hills. I haven't been out of the city for years."

"When I was very young," Anna chimed in from the back of the cart, "my parents would take us to visit a family that lived in a small village outside the city walls. I don't remember its name, but the people were very poor, even poorer than we were."

As they traveled on, passing through a little village outside the city walls they saw how poor the peasants were. "Look at those women," Priscilla said. "Some have their feet wrapped in rags. Oh, and look how thin they are, as if there wasn't enough food over the winter. What can we do to help them?" Beyond the village, they saw plowmen turning over the earth to plant the year's crops.

"It's hard breaking this ground isn't it, Father?"

"I hope the landowner is good to that man and allows him his due reward for his hard work at harvest. They often don't, so we've heard, haven't we?" Jakob said. "Let's stop here for a rest and a bit of food."

He stopped the cart, tied the horse up, and they sat along the path, enjoying their food amongst the flowers that had just opened. "Greta's salted meat and fresh bread taste very good in the open air, don't they?" Jakob mused. They sat for a time enjoying the countryside. Glancing up at the trees overhead, Jakob said, "Look at the pines in the bluffs there."

Priscilla's eyes searched the cliffs. "Those two?"

"Yes, the ones with the tops broken down, undoubtedly by the winds and storms that come to the mountains. They are broken but not destroyed, they are still rooted. They survive."

Priscilla was certain her father thought of himself and their group that way.

"Let's get moving," he said. "As good as Greta's food is, we ought to get back on the path again or we'll arrive too late. We will need to stop at Josef's cabin first."

"Where is the cabin located, Father?" Priscilla said.

"It's between Josef's land and Waldshut."

After stopping to talk to Josef, they located the cabin. It was smaller than they had hoped but adequate, and they settled in. There was a sleeping area at each end of the cabin. Jakob took the smaller of the two. Priscilla and Anna would sleep at the other end, the larger nook.

"Tomorrow we will visit Waldshut," Jakob said.

Chapter 31

Long is the way and very steep the slope
strengthen me once again, O God of Hope

"Josef tells me it's only a short distance into Waldshut. Let's walk, daughter."

Leaving Anna at the cabin to rest, Jakob and Priscilla took the narrow pathway through the tall pines toward the town.

"This warmth and sun must be a promise that spring is finally upon us. Do you think so?" Jakob asked Priscilla cheerfully.

"I do know it has come every year within my memory," Priscilla teased him.

They rounded a bend in the path and saw the small walled city.

"There it is. Let's pick up our pace. I'm looking forward to seeing this seat of freedom and meeting the people who have chosen it."

"As am I," Priscilla said.

"Josef suggested we go directly to the town hall. Hubmaier has a small room there. That's where he spends his days." Within a short walk, they saw it.

Jakob said, "There it is, on the town square, as we would expect it to be."

They walked up the steps and went inside. It wasn't as opulent as Zurich's meeting hall but adequate for a smaller village. They walked through a short hall, passing a small room with books stacked high on a little table and more on shelves lining the walls. Just behind the stack of books, they saw a man bent over a book, absorbed in his work.

"That must be him. This is a scholar's room without question," Jakob whispered. He knocked gently on the open door. "Master Hubmaier, may we have a word with you?"

Balthasar Hubmaier, a tall, older man with noble features, rose to his feet. "Master Jakob and daughter Priscilla, I have heard you would be coming for a visit. I welcome you both to Waldshut," he said with a slight bow. "Let's sit in the outer room. As you can see, there's very little sitting space here. I had to move my books here when I was recently married. Our home is small and humble; I live the life of an ex-priest and that is what it is," he said with a smile.

They judged him to be a man happy and content with his present circumstances.

"Tell me why you have come."

Jakob and Priscilla shared with him their beliefs, experiences, the renewed threats, and the new uncertainty.

"I'm sorry to hear of the turmoil in Zurich. I'm sure they wouldn't welcome my presence there either. Your story makes me even more grateful for our lives here. You have no doubt heard that we have taken control of the council and the truth of who should be baptized is now honored in Waldshut." Hubmaier smiled with a look of gratitude. "Also, we have an army that sits outside the city. Peasants who have chosen to guard us." Seeing Jakob's frown he said, "You are a pacifist, correct?"

Jakob nodded. "I do not believe in taking up arms against brothers."

"I respect your views, Jakob, but personally I believe otherwise. Perhaps if I told you my situation you would understand why. I have made an enemy of Prince Ferdinand, the Archduke of Austria. And because of my public stands, he is likely to take an even greater disliking to me because I don't back down. He may even be inclined to send the army of Austria marching this way. Therefore, I am taking precautions."

With this new information, the safety of the city came into question for Jakob and Priscilla.

Looking to find an area of agreement, Hubmaier said, "We may not agree about taking up arms, but my motto is 'Truth is Immortal,' and from what I have heard of you, I believe we agree on that. Am I correct?"

"We are in complete agreement with that motto," Jakob responded, and Priscilla nodded.

With this, Balthasar stood. "Let me take you to the hall where some meet to weave and spin their yarn. Most importantly, this is where the bible is opened, studied, and prayed over."

Within a short walk, they arrived at the hall. "What a charming old building!" Priscilla exclaimed.

"It has been here for years and used for a variety of things. Now it's a community meeting place for artisans. It's a guild of sorts and we use it—by we, I mean the community—to teach young people trades. Some are peasants who have come from the mountainside, those who have need of jobs, and those who have been displaced from their lands by the landowners. These are troubling times."

They entered the large, plain room filled with a whirl of activity: people working at looms and spinning wheels. Some stopped to look at the new faces and, being satisfied with that bit of diversion, they took up their work again.

"Very nice setup," Jakob said, looking around.

"Not as nice as your guild, I'm sure, but it works well for our needs. We gather here to work and to pray. I hope you will come to our meeting tonight." Hubmaier added quickly, as if it had just come to mind, "Jakob, I would like to invite you to speak tonight. And sister Priscilla, I have heard that you are a gifted speaker also. Would you both grace our meeting?"

"We would enjoy that immensely," Jakob answered.

With that, their plans for the evening were decided.

❧

Although this meeting was somewhat different from theirs, it was familiar enough that they felt very comfortable. They were impressed with the freedom of the people to share. At the end, many gathered around the two to ask questions about what was happening in Zurich. Priscilla answered most of the questions, so Jakob was able to talk to Balthasar.

"Sir, I was wondering, is there anything your guild needs? If I am capable, I would like to help."

"Master Jakob, we have need of more looms. If we had them, we could put more people to work."

"Then I can help. Josef mentioned this to me. I have two older looms you could have. They're smaller but in good working order. Does that suit you?"

"Most assuredly, that would be very helpful, and I thank you."

The next morning, after a good night's sleep, Jakob and Priscilla talked about the meeting. "I told Josef it's on my heart to help some in this area whose lives are hard. He suggested I visit his friend Johann, who lives farther into the mountains. He has spoken to him about our faith. He dearly loves Johann and has hope that someday he will come to embrace the Lord. He's certain if I talk to him all will be well, and Johann will come to faith. Josef surely has a great deal of confidence in me," Jakob said with a laugh.

"You do have a way with words."

Jakob sighed. "I wish the city council of Zurich felt the same. Our lives would be much different. I'm going to feed and water the little horse and get the cart ready to travel farther up into the hills this morning.

After readying the horse, Jakob started out, traveling into the hills, moving nearer to the mountains in the distance.

As he passed through a village that Josef mentioned Jakob settled in to enjoy the journey. He wasn't often this close to the mountains he loved; today he would enjoy it. Jakob closed his eyes for a moment. He breathed in the fragrance of the fir trees around him, then breathed out with pleasure. He thought of Johann and his life of pain. He bowed his head in prayer and, for a moment, the fir trees above became a chapel. What would he say to Johann? At that moment, the cart jostled. He realized the small horse needed direction, so he spoke some words of encouragement to her. With his eyes open now he watched the hills and the heights before him, considering the majesty of it all; enjoying the clean fresh air he took another deep breath and said aloud, "Ah!"

Knowing he had gone the distance Josef suggested, Jakob felt sure he was on the correct path. Josef had warned him that the horse and cart would have to be abandoned some way from the cabin. He brought the horse to a stop before a tree, climbed out of the cart with a groan or two, tied the horse and cart to the tree, and walked up the narrow footpath. Traveling higher still toward his destination, Jakob was surprised at how soon he tired. It wasn't that long ago he could walk this distance and these heights and not notice it.

There it was. He recognized the cabin from Josef's description. It stood on a high projection of rock, exposed to the winds but where the warm sun could rest upon it. And it had the advantage of the beauty of the valley below. Jakob thought that despite its humbleness, it had a charm about it. Just then, a voice startled Jakob. "What are you staring at?"

At the side of the cabin he saw a man of about sixty who looked tired and sat resting on a tree stump taking in the sun. Jakob moved closer and said, "Hello friend—"

"How do you call me friend? We have never met."

Remembering Josef's warning that Johann was disagreeable at times, Jakob took another approach. "I am a friend of Josef, our common friend. He told me he comes regularly to visit. He hoped I could meet with you today in his place."

"Humph. I suppose you are one of those religious ones. I've told him I am not of that camp, but he continues to come anyway."

"Perhaps we can find common ground and other interests. I'm certain you will want to extend hospitality to a weary traveler. I'm more winded than I'd expected."

"Perhaps. I suppose it's good to converse with others. You look like a person from the city. Am I wrong?" he said, looking Jakob up and down.

"That I am. I'm from Zurich."

Johann rose slowly from the stump and walked with a bit of a limp to the cabin. Turning to Jakob he said gruffly, "Come inside then. My home is humble, but it suits my needs."

Entering the cabin, Jakob saw what he meant. It was very simple. The only furniture was a table, two chairs, and in one corner, a bed. In the other corner sat a cupboard with a few dishes on a wooden shelf. It was humble but comfortable.

"Take a spot by the fire and warm yourself," Johann said gruffly. The fire was in full blaze and Jakob was glad for its warmth. It was cooler this far into the mountains. He rubbed his hands as he sat before the fire, looked into it, and watched its mesmerizing dance. He forgot himself for a while and was startled again when Johann asked, "Would you like something to eat?"

"Yes, I'm hungry after my trip."

They fell into conversation and found a pleasant rhythm of agreement about the history of Switzerland. After a while Jakob asked, "I would like very much to repay your hospitality. Is there anything I could do for you, Johann? We have had a lively and pleasing conversation."

Once again, Johann looked with suspicion upon his guest. Then, breathing heavily, he said, "I was once a man who lived a better life. I had sheep I took to market in Zurich. Now I am unable to do that because of my age. I have a grandson who has the heart to take this over, but he doesn't have a market. I have lost my contacts in Zurich." And so, an agreement was formed between them.

❧

"We parted as friends," Jakob told Priscilla later in the day as she and Anna greeted him at the cabin.

"You must be tired, Papa." Priscilla looked at him with concern, seeing his weariness.

"I just need to sit a while," he said as she helped him out of his coat.

"We are making dinner. Tell us how it went."

"I didn't get to talk to him about the Lord. There didn't seem an opportunity for it, but we had a most pleasant time, and I will visit him again. Perhaps we will talk more, and I will have an opportunity then."

❧

Chapter 32

I hear Thee in the silence of the mountains

Later in the month, Priscilla and Jakob traveled the dusty path back toward Zurich. Although the future was uncertain, they had decided to make the best of the trip home, determined to enjoy it.

As they drove along, enduring the ruts in the rough road, Priscilla enjoyed the gentle breeze that fanned her face. She watched the sun's light flicker through the branches of the trees ahead and listened to the birds singing what she thought of as an ancient melody, passing their music back and forth between them. She wished she could see them. Just then, a flock of birds flew in front of the slow-moving cart. *How did they follow each other so closely, as if they had planned it? Their flight was like a dance,* she thought, *a mysterious, eternal dance.* She wondered at the mystery and admired the harmony before her.

She considered her father's relationship with the magistrate, thinking it, too, was a kind of dance. He tried again and again to achieve an understanding—but there was no harmony in that dance.

Jakob broke into her thoughts. "Priscilla, do you ever think of the mountains being born?"

"How do you see that happening, Papa?" she said, with delight in her voice. She sat back and waited for his answer.

Jakob, reins in hand, urged the horse on, as he replied. "I think God laid His finger on the earth and a great and mighty roar rose up. The earth began to open and in time, majestic mountains were born. When He saw what He had done, He was jubilant, and He decided to make more." He glanced at her, his face aglow.

Priscilla peered down the road, imagining it. "I like that image, Father. Do you wish you had been there?"

"Sometimes I hear that roar when I am among the peaks, and I remember God and His might."

"You don't think He just spoke them into existence?"

"I like to think He wanted a direct hand in creating the mountains. He wanted to use His finger to touch the earth to add to its beauty. And in doing so He gave us their beauty to enjoy." They rode along quietly for a time, passing through the mist over the hills and enjoying the steady sound of the horse's hooves meeting the ground.

Priscilla broke the silence, "I think the Lord loves the mountains and they are special to Him. As scripture says, 'He treads the high places of the earth.' Do you want to know what I've always thought of the mountains?"

He nodded.

"When I was a child standing on the streets of Zurich, I would look out over the mountains surrounding the city and think of them as the end of the world. I would think of their size and majesty, and I would imagine they were like guardians standing at attention. Soldiers on the ready—sturdy, and vigilant, waiting to protect us." She sighed heavily.

Unaware of her distress because he was lost in thought, Jakob said, "He is the one who stoops down to look on the heavens and the earth, as the scripture says. What if He stands on the mountains that we see, and He looks upon us to care for us?"

"I hope He does," Priscilla said. She hurriedly added, "I know He does. He looks upon us, He cares for us, and always has. But I'm worried about what we will face in the city."

"I know." He patted her hand and lifted the reins to give the horse the message to hurry along. "We will face it with the courage our Lord gives us. 'For the Lord is the great God, the great King above all gods. In His hand are the depths of the earth, and the mountain peaks belong to Him.'"

Priscilla continued with the scripture, "'The sea is His, for He made it, and his hands formed the dry land.'" Priscilla laughed. "We still remember that scripture that we memorized so long ago. Maybe you are right, and God did use His finger."

"I like to imagine it that way." Then Jakob grew serious. "I've been thinking, we have lived all our lives in the safety of the valley, surrounded by the mountains. But when one travels into the mountains, it's a different story. Sometimes choices are taken out of the hands of the traveler and the mountains become the decision-makers. Sometimes decisions about life and death are not in the hands of the traveler. Knowing this reminds us to put our trust in the Lord, does it not?"

As the city came into view, Priscilla exclaimed, "There it is, our lovely city. Doesn't it look beautiful? We haven't seen it from this aspect in a while." *Beautiful, but perhaps no longer a friend,* she thought.

Jakob pulled the horse up to the front of the house. They sat for a time looking at it. Priscilla said, "I love the house, don't you, Papa? Should I walk to Greta's and ask her to come and cook for us tonight?"

"Let's live our lives as if nothing has changed," Jakob said. Then, with enthusiasm, he said, "I'm off to the guild to see how it has fared under Michael's leadership."

As Jakob stepped into the familiar hall he heard, "Welcome, Master Jakob."

"Michael, how has it been, your season as the Master of the guild?"

"I believe it has gone well. You will have to ask the others for their opinion," he said lightheartedly.

"I would expect nothing less, Michael. You are very capable."

"I would add one thing." Michael looked around to ensure no one was close enough to hear. "A councilman has been around several times while you were gone. He looked more and more severe each time he visited." Michael's eyes held an unspoken question.

"Let's not worry about the council today, Michael. Our only concern will be the work. By the way, have you seen those two older looms?"

"The two that were used years ago?"

Jakob nodded.

"I believe they have been stored in the small closet in Remy's room. Wait till you see how many shoes Remy has hung, ready to be distributed. He's been like a madman, working day and night."

Jakob stepped into Remy's room and saw five hanging lines full of newly made shoes and two bags in a corner. Jakob looked at Remy proudly as he appraised the shoes nearest to him. "Excellent workmanship, Remy. They are even finer than the earlier ones you made. Not that those weren't good! But these are beautiful."

"That's partly because the leather I've gotten from the new tanner is excellent. Beautiful color and quality," Remy said, studying the shoes on the table in front of him.

"When these are dry and ready to go," Jakob said, "you should bag them up, add them to those other two bags in the corner, borrow the cart, and take them to Waldshut. There is great need there and in the smaller communities around the town." Remy raised his eyebrows and stood looking at Jakob. "And then you could see Anna," Jakob added, having seen how Remy looked at her and knowing his feelings toward her.

"They will be ready tomorrow. I'll leave straight away," Remy said.

Jakob smiled. *Young love, how sweet to be a part of it.*

❧

Priscilla trod the rough cobblestones to Greta's house, a path she had taken many times. But today, people greeted her differently. Some responded awkwardly to her hellos. Others turned away when they recognized her. Still others looked at her with disdain. The most hurtful was her friend and neighbor, Bella. She turned her head, ignored Priscilla's greeting, and hurried away.

Greta met her at the door. "Come in, mistress. I heard you were back in town, so I'm prepared to work today." As she got her coat, she looked uneasy.

As they began walking up the hill, Greta turned toward Priscilla and said, "Mistress, they say such awful things about you and Master Jakob. I try defending you, but I am just one voice, and they are many."

Priscilla heard the sadness in her voice. "Thank you, Greta," she said, "for your care and concern. It means much to us. Let's hurry." Priscilla looked down as she walked, unwilling to meet any more condemning faces. She thought others' attitudes were something she and her father must bear now that they were considered outsiders.

❧

"Remy!" Anna answered the door. "What brings you to Waldshut?"

"You," he said quietly, looking into her eyes. He added quickly, "I mean, Jakob wanted me to deliver the shoes I've finished. Want to see what I brought?" He gestured toward the cart overflowing with bags.

"So many!" she said with excitement. "You have been a very busy man," she said as she walked to the cart looking with admiration at his cache.

"Could I stay awhile?" Remy said shyly. "Maybe we could catch up. I haven't seen you for a long time." His eyes took her in. "You're just as beautiful as I remembered."

"Remy, you lie!" she said, smiling despite her attempt to be serious. "I'm due to have the baby next month." She rubbed her stomach. "I don't know how you would say that." She shook her head with amusement.

"Could we talk? There is something I wanted to ask you."

"I won't invite you into the cabin, it wouldn't be proper," she said, scanning the path to the town. "Let's sit here." She pointed to a rough-hewn bench outside the cabin door.

They sat and he turned toward her. "There's something I've been thinking about. I've thought about this over and over in my head." Remy spoke with increasing intensity, and Anna waited patiently for him to continue. "Anna, I want to marry you. We could marry and tell people that the baby is mine." Remy began speaking even more rapidly. "I would take care of you. I have work now, so that wouldn't be a problem, you know." He stopped, looking deep into her eyes. "Or we could move to another town where no one knows us, and we could start a new life there." Anna sat with her eyes focused on Remy. Finally, Remy said, "You're not saying anything."

"Remy, it's not that easy." She was still for a time. "The thing is, Remy," she paused, wondering what he would think and continued, "The thing is, I think I still have feelings for Fredrik . . . and this is his baby."

Remy looked at her as if he had been stabbed. Shooting up, he said hastily, "I'll be going then."

"Remy! Don't just walk off. We should talk about this."

Remy walked away as if he hadn't heard Anna. He sprang into the cart and headed into Waldshut.

The next morning Remy stormed into the guild hall, causing enough noise that everyone stopped to watch. Remy carried a large bag into his area in the back room.

Something's wrong here, Jakob thought as he watched Remy angrily march through the guild. It's not what he had expected after Remy's time with Anna. Jakob followed him into the back room. "Remy, what's happening? What are you doing?"

"I'm leaving."

Jakob watched as Remy flung his tools into his bag.

"Does this have anything to do with Anna?"

"I'm joining the peasant army again, those surrounding Waldshut. If I can't marry her, I can at least protect her," he said. He charged out of the building with Jakob staring after him.

"I've done so well at keeping my anxieties in check, but this morning seems to have brought them all back," Priscilla said to her father. "And now Remy leaving so unexpectedly."

"It has something to do with Anna," Jakob responded. "Priscilla, I have an idea. We have been too involved in life's struggles lately. We need time away from them, time with our music. Let us put our hand to our instruments tonight, it will bring us consolation."

Later, after dinner was served and eaten, Priscilla prepared the area by pulling up chairs and music stands. She took up her flute, and her father his viola, and they began to play. Soon, the music worked itself into their hearts. They were well into a piece when Jakob looked up to see Greta listening as she stood in the doorway.

"Greta, come join us. Sit here." He got up to put a chair near them. "There, that's the perfect place."

"Oh no, master," she said, feeling uncomfortable being asked into the family area. "I have work to do in the kitchen." She turned to leave.

"No, it can wait. Sit and enjoy yourself with us. Let us know if we were doing well."

"I know nothing of this skill," she said shyly, clearly feeling awkward with the familiarity required of her. "I only enjoy what I hear coming from your hands."

They urged her, and finally, she joined in as a spectator. After a time, Priscilla looked over to see Greta lay her head back, close her eyes, and tap out the beat with her fingers on the arm of the chair. Priscilla glanced at her father and smiled, glad that their loyal friend was enjoying the music.

Chapter 33

*The burning winds have blown away
the soft, blue mist of yesterday*

Running his hands over the wooden frames, Jakob examined the older looms, remembering their faithful years of service. *Yes, they are workable*, he thought, *and they will be a blessing to someone in Waldshut.* They would have a new home there, as possibly would he and Priscilla. Glancing at the area that had been Remy's, he puzzled over unanswered questions. He said out loud, "What happened?"

"Are you talking to yourself now, Jakob?" William said, walking into the room with a big smile.

"Oh yes. I talk to myself, especially lately, when no one else listens to me," he said with a wry smile and a chuckle.

"I didn't know if I would find you here today," William said.

"It's good to see you, friend. Do you have time to take a seat?"

Looking around the room, William asked, "Is Remy not working these days?"

"It is a long story. I'll fill you in sometime." The two sat down and Jakob started. "Priscilla and I have traveled to Waldshut. We are looking at our options." Hearing Priscilla's name, William's eyes brightened. Jakob continued, "I feel we must look to the future. It is not particularly safe here in Zurich these days."

"I see many of the community have left the city, especially those with new babies and small children," William said.

"They had little choice," Jakob agreed with resignation. "We have many trials and tribulations on this earth. But we also have many blessings and I think of them often. We have had a rich life here in Zurich and many good memories. They are alive to me, William, the memories I mean. I choose to think on the good." For a moment Jakob closed his eyes.

"Not everyone has left the city. One comes to mind, and that would be Felix." William said.

"Felix!" Jakob opened his eyes and sat upright.

"I saw him preaching in front of the old church."

"Felix! I haven't seen him in months. The brother is so daring to continue preaching in the city." Jakob's eyes grew bright thinking about the young men and their bravery. "It's not safe for him here," Jakob added.

William shook his head. "We will see what comes of it." They talked for a time before William had to leave.

Jakob hurried home to tell Priscilla William's news. He found her peering over her vegetable garden. *She probably won't be planting her beloved garden this year,* he thought. Disappointment for her crept into his heart. Priscilla looked up at her father. "You are home early. Is everything all right?"

"William saw Felix preaching at the old church again."

Priscilla drew in her breath and leaned against the fence. "I hope he doesn't come by here. They are still watching us. I have seen them again," she said anxiously.

Later that evening, after Priscilla had gone to bed, Jakob leaned into the candlelight reading a treasured book when a soft knock came at the door. It startled Jakob. *Who could it be?* As he set down his book, a second soft knock came. He walked to the door and opened it and he found Felix standing in the doorway.

"Come in, quickly, brother." They paused inside the door to look fondly at each other and embrace. With emotion, Jakob said, "I didn't think I would ever see you again, Felix. Let me call Priscilla."

Hurriedly, Felix said, "No, I can't stay, Jakob. You can imagine how I must keep moving. I am the greater enemy now. I wanted to stop to say I'm all right and still preaching the gospel."

"We heard you were at your old post in front of the Gross Muenster." Jakob placed his hands on Felix's shoulders and said, as if to bless him, "I'm proud of you, Felix."

"You have been a father to me, Jakob. I'll never forget it." With a sense of urgency, Felix said," I must go. Say hello to dear Priscilla. Both of you have always meant much to me." With that, he was gone.

The next morning Jakob and Priscilla were in the kitchen when a forceful knock came at the door. Greta stood at the fireplace paralyzed with fear. Seeing her expression, Jakob said, "I'll answer it, Greta." He opened the door to see William with an uncharacteristic look of distress.

"They have Felix in the prison."

"Felix in prison? And you saw him just yesterday, Papa?" Priscilla said as they sat at the table hours later, trying to make sense of these new events. "What shall we do?"

"You will do nothing," he said with determination. "I am going to visit him this afternoon."

"I should go with you!"

"It is not safe. The jail is an unfit place for a woman to visit and I don't know what I will find there. Perhaps he has been beaten. No. I will go alone and that's final."

Jakob walked slowly toward Wellenberg prison, uneasy about what he might see. He stopped in front of the prison walls and looked up at them wondering where they might be holding Felix. Felix, the scholar, and the son of the chief canon of the oldest, most prestigious church in Zurich. Where does a jailor hold someone like him? Once again, he marveled at Felix's fortitude.

"I'm here to see Felix Manz."

The guard looked Jakob up and down and said with scorn, "Felix Manz, the heretic. Wait here." He walked out of the room and Jakob waited patiently. A different jailer came to

Jakob. "Follow me," he said curtly. They passed through a series of heavy doors. Each time a door was slammed behind Jakob, his stomach tightened a little more. It was the finality of that sound. He knew he could easily become a prisoner here himself. How would he face that?

As they went deeper into the prison, he noticed it was getting darker and danker. He steeled his heart for what he would see when he finally reached his friend.

"He is here. Felix Manz, you have a visitor." The cell door was opened for Jakob and loudly slammed behind him.

Jakob glanced about at Felix's dismal circumstances. No bed was provided, just a small straw-covered mat on the floor. He asked, "Brother, how goes it?"

"As you can see, I didn't make it out of the city as I had planned. Some of the council's men apprehended me before I made it out of the walls."

"I suppose they were watching our house. Are you discouraged, my son?"

"I am not, Jakob. On the contrary, I am very encouraged and have decided not to allow my soul to be downcast. I rejoice in God even in this forsaken place." Felix glanced around his cell and then back to Jakob. Felix smiled, and Jakob saw his tranquility.

"That eases my heart a great deal."

"I am at peace, and I feel I have walked the path that was meant for me. I obeyed God, and not man, and now I trust Him for the outcome." Jakob nodded his approval. "They have allowed me my bible while here. This is what I read this morning: 'The Lord is good to those whose hope is in Him, to the one who seeks Him, it is good to wait quietly for the salvation of the Lord.' So, I wait."

After leaving the prison, Jakob walked to the guild. He saw clouds begin to roll in from the mountains and lamented that he hadn't brought a coat to protect him from the rain they promised. As he drew closer to the hall, he was puzzled to see a placard on the door. Coming closer he read, "Closed until further notice by proclamation of the City Council" with a large signature of the magistrate.

It had happened, what he feared had come upon him. He could appeal this, but to whom? He had no freedom in this matter. He walked home as the rain pelted him. Now he wasn't thinking about the forgotten coat but rather what his imagination posed about the future.

Entering his home, it came to him, and he knew what they must do. Just then, there was a knock at the door. Jakob opened it to find William there. He was winded and hurried through the door, saying frantically, "Jakob, you and Priscilla need to leave the city at once. The council has plans to confiscate your home tomorrow. They have already taken the guild."

"Yes, I know." Jakob's expression was weary.

"They are signing proclamations to jail you . . . and Priscilla."

"My plan is to leave tomorrow early . . ."

"No, Jakob. You must leave today, immediately. They are coming for you."

"What did you say?" Priscilla came hurrying into the room. "Did you say we must leave today?" She looked at her father, her eyes full of fear.

They thanked William. He left and they hurriedly packed their things. Since there wasn't much room in the cart, they were taking the minimum they could fit. Had there been more time, they could have borrowed another, larger cart. How do you choose what's most important among those things you have loved for years? Priscilla decided to take two small statues that were her mother's and wrapped them carefully. They needed more cooking pans and utensils at the cabin. There was only the bare minimum.

"We are counting on Josef letting us stay at the cabin, aren't we?" she asked Jakob as she added the pots to the cart and then climbed up into it.

"I'm certain we will have a place there," Jakob said confidently as he slowly climbed into the cart. They sat for a moment looking at the house they both loved so much. "I have lived in that house my entire life," she mused. "So many happy memories of childhood and those who have come and gone. She thought of her mother, her husband, and her two children, all gone so quickly. She thought of the cooks and the housekeepers, how they had added color to their lives. Good food, order, and love. And the times of fellowship that were shared around the scripture with brothers and sisters.

Then reality was upon them. They looked up to see some of the magistrate's men on foot, hurrying toward them. Her father picked up the reins and commanded the horse to hurry. They took off down the street heading for the walls of the city. He pushed the little horse more than it was accustomed to being driven. Both of their hearts were beating hard.

"Priscilla, look back at them," her father said breathlessly. "Are any of them on horses?"

Priscilla turned to look, and she said, "No. One is yelling and shaking his fist, but none of them are mounted."

"Good, we will be out of the city soon." He again commanded the horse to pick up its speed.

Once the two were beyond the walls and far enough outside the city, they felt danger was behind them. Yet Priscilla felt a tension deep in her heart, an unwanted companion that visited her again as they traveled away from her home. As she listened to the steady trotting of the horse against the hard path, she felt as if something was being poured out of her; she felt an emptiness. As if her father heard her thoughts, he spoke: "There will be a new life waiting for us when we get to Waldshut, my dear." He paused. "We have lived a hidden life, a quiet one before the young men came into our group, but then we entered a new era. It was time for change. We felt it. Our friends—Jorg with his big, formidable ways, his loud voice, and Felix and Conrad—they burst open the confines of our little group, they came with fire. I remember Conrad's words, they were so alive. It was as if we no longer had our feet upon the earth. There was a flow to it, and it seemed to carry us and it changed us. We were like wineskins that burst and new wine came forth."

Priscilla listened to her father, but she didn't feel the same reassurance. She didn't want to be that wineskin. *Why couldn't it have continued as it was?*

Jakob went on, "We loved our quiet life. Then that faint call, that still small voice. The call to join the saints who had come before us." He looked at Priscilla and said, "And those that will follow us. And now, like the saints of old, we are experiencing suffering. But we will honor God by trusting Him in our day of trouble."

As they bounced along the path toward their new home, Priscilla tried to find a place of peace for her empty heart. She went to the Lord in prayer and stayed there quietly before Him.

"We are about halfway to the cabin and the horse needs a rest. Let's stop and eat some of the salted meat you packed for us." Stepping away from the cart felt good for both of them. They were stiff from the journey. "It feels good to stretch. Let's sit by this little stream to water the horse," Jakob said. The horse was tied to a small tree near the creek, and Jakob wearily sat down. Priscilla unpacked their lunch from the back of the cart and carried it to where they would sit. She sat down in discouragement on a rock by the mountain stream and began to eat some of the meat and bread. They had followed this stream for a time, and it had become a companion. She watched the creek tumbling and whispering as it flowed down a little waterfall, meandering away to its unknown destination.

Priscilla sat watching the little creek, thinking, and praying. She sighed, turned toward Jakob, and said, "Somehow the little creek is comforting me, Papa. God's creation I suppose. He can use anything."

Jakob leaned back into the grass for a short nap. When he awoke, he said, "Let's go, Priscilla. We need to be on our way. It's getting late and we won't want to be traveling at night. The road is unfamiliar to me."

As they continued farther into the hills approaching Waldshut, a mist began to fall, enveloping them. They were unable to see more than five feet in front of the cart. Priscilla looked at her father. She saw his lips moving just a bit. She knew he was praying, and asked him, "Does this not worry you, Father?"

"I must admit I feel a tension."

Priscilla could feel his anxiety. Yet after a time, peace settled upon them again and they began to see the mist from a different perspective.

Priscilla said, "The mist is beginning to be a teacher to me."

"How so?" Jakob wondered what she was thinking.

"It is reminding me of how the presence of God is all around us. God is so big, He fills the whole earth, but we don't see Him, and we forget this. The mist is a reminder. It is enough for us to see only the next few steps. The Lord goes before and is making a way for us."

Chapter 34

Jakob brought the cart to a halt in front of the cabin. Priscilla said, "I hope Anna is doing well."

"Let's empty the cart and I'll get the horse settled in the barn," he replied.

Priscilla carried an armful of her things into the cabin, calling out, "Anna, we are back." There was no answer and she stared at dishes from the last meal sitting unattended on the table. "Anna . . . ?"

"I'm here, Priscilla, on the bed."

Priscilla pulled aside the curtain. Anna was bent over with a hand on her abdomen, obviously in pain. Anna looked up at her and said, "I think the baby is coming."

Priscilla asked, "When did the pains start?"

"About mid-day."

"Did you call the midwife?"

"No, I did not."

"I thought you were going to call her."

"I was, Priscilla. It's just that it came on so fast and you weren't here and . . . well, the real answer is I want you to deliver the baby. I wanted you all along. Please say you will."

Priscilla looked with love into the young face she cared so deeply for. She knew she couldn't say no. "I will, of course, deliver your baby." She shook her head, attempting to hide the smile that was taking control of her face. "How are you feeling overall?"

"Pretty good," Anna said. She grinned and added, "Of course, when the pains come, it's not much fun."

Priscilla laughed. "That's just a part of the process."

"Will you stay with me through it all?" Anna put her hand on her abdomen and bent over again. "Here comes another pain."

Priscilla sat next to her and said, "Take my hand."

Anna took it. She grimaced and groaned. When the contraction was over, she said, "I feel better now that you're here holding my hand."

"Good, I will continue to hold that hand." She patted it. "I'll be with you for the entire labor. I'm not going anywhere. We are in this together. We will work to bring this little one into the world."

"I'm so glad you will be delivering my baby." Anna looked at Priscilla earnestly. "So glad." She sighed. "I always wanted you. And somehow, I knew you would be the one, though you insisted you wouldn't be. Oh, here comes another pain." She gripped Priscilla's hand hard.

Priscilla said. "I want you to concentrate on relaxing and sort of riding the pains."

"All right."

Priscilla knew from the level of Anna's grip she would have to remind her again. "Later on, I'll have an herbal remedy to help you along, but for the time being, we will work on relaxing. Are you excited to see your baby, Anna?"

"I'm so looking forward to holding little Barbara."

Priscilla smiled at Anna's confidence that it would be a girl. She hoped Anna wouldn't be disappointed.

"I'm going to get my herbal supplies together and then we'll get you ready for this delivery."

"Yes, I'm patient. Is there anything you need help with?"

"No, you just rest. It's going to be some time before we see that baby."

Priscilla hurried to her trunk that held the things she moved from Zurich. She felt a sense of discomfort and nervous energy. It had been such a long time since she had attended a birth. Fear gripped her. *What was she doing? Was this a mistake?* Her last experience, with the magistrate's wife, raced through her thoughts. She needed to focus. She didn't want to let the past interfere now. She dug deep into the trunk. Her midwifery bags were at the very bottom, packed tightly. She brought them out and stared at them. She'd thought she would never use them again, yet there was that little feeling that maybe she would. The fear returned. *Had it been too long? Would she remember what was needed today?*

She clasped her hands together and bowed her head for a time. Looking up, she glanced at Anna, who was waiting patiently for her. She knew Anna trusted her completely; it gave her courage.

She arranged the needed herbs on the table in the middle of the small cabin. Walking toward Anna, she stopped before her and said, "Are you ready?"

❧

"We are now people without a home, Josef. I mean Anna, my daughter, and I," Jakob said as he and Josef walked to a meeting of the brethren.

Speaking earnestly, Josef said, "You are welcome to stay at the cabin for as long as you need. I hope you know that. It is my pleasure to serve an honorable person such as yourself, Jakob. You and your daughter will bring much to the community with your wisdom and bible knowledge. You are a very welcome addition. Balthasar agrees and has said as much."

"And life for us goes on," Jakob replied with a smile. "A new baby will come into this world tonight."

"Anna?"

"Yes, and I am glad we are here in this safe haven."

Josef nodded. "She will not have the decision about baptism she would have had in Zurich."

As they neared the meeting place, the two nodded in greeting toward a passing man. He looked away with angry disregard. When they had put enough distance between the man and themselves, Josef spoke up. "I have noticed," he said, "and maybe you have also, that with some angry people, the real problem is that they hate themselves. I am schooling myself to remember that when I meet one."

They considered this. Then, in chorus, they looked at each other and said, "Johann!"

"We must visit him again," Jakob said quickly. "We will go tomorrow."

The next day, the horse and cart went as far as a cart could carry them on the rough mountainous paths. They then climbed on foot. Josef watched as Jakob struggled to climb the last distance, several times stopping to catch his breath. Finally, they reached the beautiful spot where the humble cabin jutted out on the rocks.

After Johann greeted them at the door of the cabin, they sat inside listening to his stories, and sharing some light conversation. Finally, Jakob said, "Your home is very isolated from others. Are you happy here?"

"I am indeed happy here. It's a place where I can hear myself think, far from the crowds, far from the endless chatter," he said with a dismissive gesture.

Jakob observed Johann and thought he didn't see happiness. A picture of the broken trees he had seen on the mountainside came to him. Now he saw a lonely, bitter man who had suffered hardships, one who had been battered by life's disappointments and afflictions. Looking deeper, he thought he observed a heart that was hard but one that might have a crack, an opening where, just maybe, a well-placed word might be a key to opening that heart.

He said, "I have come with a story to tell you, Johann. Are you interested?"

"I like a good story and I will listen." Johann settled back into his chair, ready for the tale.

Jakob began his story, the one he had told Priscilla about his hard heart toward God and his parents, his drunkenness, and his greed. He talked about the times he had struggles with God. He told it all, some of it raw.

Johann looked hard and long at Jakob. "Is this story true?"

"Yes, every word." Jakob nodded toward Johann.

"You don't look like you would have been that person. It's hard to believe." Johann continued looking intently at Jakob.

"It is my story. I've been changed by the man, Jesus. I now have peace. What about you? Don't you want peace in your life? Do you have burdens you want to lay down?"

"The man Jesus! I remember the stories told of him in our little village church." Bitterness returned to his voice. "A man, meek and mild. That story means nothing to a man like me," he said forcefully. "I have known the hardest of times. What do I care about him, this Jesus?"

Josef took up the story from there. "Let me tell you, Johann, Jesus was a man's man. I see you haven't heard the full story. There's more. He stood up to the religious leaders of the time who were heaping unfair laws on the people, laws that they were unable to follow. He stood up to them, the powerful, the rich, and the wealthy. And the people, those just like you and me, loved him for it. He was strong and did not back down. And for this, he died."

"And that's the end of the story. He failed!"

"No, it wasn't the end. He came back to life."

Johann said, "How?"

"You know the story. What happened on Easter." Josef said.

Josef and Jakob looked squarely at Johann, and they saw a change, something in his face, a softening.

After a pause, and because Johann wasn't a man easily swayed, he said, "You have given me much to think about. Come again and we will talk more."

Chapter 35

Feeling deeply tired after his time in the mountains with Johann and Josef, Jakob opened the door to the cabin and heard a wail from inside. A smile overtook him, and with it, the weariness was carried away. "What do I hear? Have we added to the brethren today?" he said as he walked in.

Priscilla hurried out of the bedroom to greet her father. "It's a girl. Do you remember how Anna said all along it would be a girl? She calls her Barbara, after our dear friend. Come and see." Priscilla motioned for Jakob to follow her. She drew back the curtain surrounding the bed. Anna was propped up by pillows, holding her newborn. She smiled with pride as she looked at Jakob. "See, Jakob, what's come about while you were gone?"

"A new little one to love," Jakob said, gazing at the baby. "I suppose our lives will be different from this time forward."

Little Barbara let out a cry to affirm it.

Priscilla laughed. "It's dinner time. We will let Mama take care of that. Papa, come sit down, you must be hungry after your trip."

"I am, I've had only a bit to eat at Johann's cabin today."

"I have some very tasty fowl for you. I cooked it earlier." Priscilla brought him a dish. "I want to hear about your talk with the mountain man," she said eagerly.

Jakob shared the earlier conversation with Priscilla. "I felt when we were done talking, Johann's heart was open to the Lord; that was our goal."

As the evening shadows deepened into night, candles were lit around the cabin. The night was filled with cooing over the little one. It was a perfect ending to a good day.

The next day Priscilla and Jakob talked while Anna and the little one slept. "Our days have been filled with such dread lately, Papa. Today was different and I'm relishing it," Priscilla mused.

"I pray that our lives here in Waldshut will be a blessing to others," Jakob added. Just then, someone pounded at the door.

"I'll answer it, it's probably Josef," Jakob said, wondering at the violence of the blows. He opened the door, and it became clear. "Jorg, Conrad. You two are a sight for sore eyes. Please come in."

Priscilla jumped up to greet them, and Jorg, in his usual bombastic way, began talking too loudly. "Quiet, Jorg. We have a sleeping baby now."

Answering loudly and excitedly, Jorg said, "Anna's baby?"

"Jorg!"

The big man looked chastised. He whispered, "The baby came? When can we see it?"

Walking out of the sleeping area, Anna said, "Jorg, Conrad, you're here. It's been too long." She was holding the baby, who was sleeping soundly despite the commotion.

Jorg and Conrad gathered around the baby. Conrad said, "She's beautiful, Anna."

Jorg laughed. "Of course, she is, Conrad, look at the mama."

"And you named her Barbara after my wife," Conrad said wistfully. "I wish she were here. She would be so honored. I haven't seen her for weeks."

"Where is she, Conrad?" Anna said.

"With friends outside the city, and she is safe. I am at peace with it," Conrad said softly.

Unable to contain himself, Jorg exclaimed, "We have good news to share. Felix is with us!"

"What?" Jakob said. "I visited him in prison. He's not there now?"

"Conrad and I helped him escape. He's back preaching in the towns around Zurich."

Jakob and Priscilla looked stunned. "Tell us more," Jakob said.

Conrad took up the story. "Jorg and I heard he had been imprisoned at Wellenberg. So we hatched a plan. We knew it would be hard to get into the prison, so we decided to go in as monks. Jorg knew the head jailer as someone who was sympathetic to the Catholic way and who was quite a drinker. We dressed in robes Jorg had from his time in the monastery.

Oh, and, by the way, it doesn't look like Remy stays at our house. What's that about?"

"That's another long story for later. Go on."

"We got into the prison and brought with us a jug of wine."

Jakob looked at them, shocked. Conrad knew he probably didn't approve. "We had to get the brother out of that place, Jakob. I know that prisons aren't pleasant places but the conditions there were horrible. It was dirty and dank, it stank, and we saw rats. We wondered if they were feeding him well." Conrad continued, "We talked with the jailer for a time, our robes and hoods protecting our identities in that dark place. We gave him the wine. I think he had already been drinking, evidence being the empty bottle sitting around."

Jorg could wait no longer for Conrad to get to the end. He broke in, "We sat outside the cell and visited with Felix for a time, then I walked down to where the jailer was. Just as I suspected, he was asleep. I took the keys. We got Felix out, and we left in the boat docked outside the prison."

"What did you do with the keys?"

Jorg chuckled. "Threw them in the river, where else!"

Jakob shook his head. "I suppose that is one of the few uses of alcohol I can condone."

"It worked like a charm, he drank about half of the jug, and he was out."

Priscilla exclaimed, "What a story!"

"What were you saying about Remy earlier?" Jorg asked.

"Hush, Jorg, Anna may hear," Priscilla whispered, looking toward Anna's sleeping area where she had returned. "He left Zurich to join the peasant armies. We are not sure why. We think it had something to do with Anna," Priscilla said, whispering again.

"Anna turned him down when he asked to marry her, that's why," Jorg said.

Conrad said, "How would you know? You haven't seen either of them for months."

"I just know things sometimes," Jorg whispered. "He loves Anna."

Conrad raised his eyebrows and shrugged his shoulders. "It's true, Jorg does know things at times, and I'm always surprised."

"We have other exciting news," Conrad said eagerly, standing up straight, as if to announce something. "We have been preaching with great success in the small towns around the city. Preaching and baptizing many new believers. Once the weather broke this spring, we began in earnest, going from town to town. People were ready to receive because of their discouragement with the peasant wars. Their hearts were open and ready to hear. We preached that the true church could only be formed by those gripped by God's spirit. They heard and believed. Palm Sunday, we baptized the largest number of converts ever in the time we've been preaching."

"Wonderful, excellent news!" Jakob looked at the two young men with pride. They had come so far, especially Jorg. "What an accomplishment—and on Palm Sunday. That makes it even more notable."

Conrad added, "Now we will have to raise up men in the town as elders for the new churches that are being formed. We thought we would talk to Josef about how to do that."

"Excellent idea," Jakob said. "You will need to talk to him if you wish to stay the night in Waldshut. He will have ideas for places for you to sleep and on how to proceed."

Chapter 36

As Priscilla readied porridge for breakfast, she sang to herself. It was a song Barbara had sung in their meetings in her beautiful voice. Anna, with the baby in her arms, pushed the curtain aside from her sleeping area.

Priscilla looked up. "Oh, I'm sorry. Was I too loud?"

"It was time for me to get up, and the baby can sleep through almost anything."

Priscilla set two bowls of steaming porridge and goat milk on the table. "Come, sit down, and talk to me. How do you feel?"

Anna looked down at the sleeping baby in her lap. She said to Priscilla, "It's come as a great surprise, how I feel having this baby come into my life. I have such a fierce love for her. I feel I would do anything for her—anything to protect her." She added, "What about you, Priscilla? Was it hard to take up the midwifery again?"

"That has been my surprise. How pleasant it is to be back at my old work. It was wonderful to welcome new life into the world again. That's one aspect of midwifery that I especially enjoyed."

"Will you take it up again then?"

"That is my intention, God willing. I'm even planning my new herb garden and what I will need to use for birthing."

Interrupting them, Jakob walked through the front door and said, "It's beautifully warm outside today. Let me take the little one and sit in the sun." With conviction, he added, "She will like it."

"I believe you speak for yourself, Jakob," Anna said, smiling at him.

"I do, but little Barbara agrees with me." He picked up the baby. "You'll find baby and me sitting behind the cabin."

The women watched as he walked outside.

"He seems sad these days," Priscilla said, looking concerned. "He doesn't have his old pursuits to give his attention to. I suppose he doesn't have the same feeling of purpose." Then, looking at the porridge, she said, "We should eat before it gets too cold."

❧

That day was the beginning of changes in Jakob. He spent more time indoors, no longer took his daily walks, and began sleeping often during the day, which had never been his habit. Some days while he slept, Priscilla sat beside him, holding his hand, worrying and praying. He drifted in and out of sleep, and she wondered at the peace that seemed to surround him.

But one day, he woke up like a new man, one with a new strength and vigor. Sitting at the breakfast table, he was dressed in the clothes that he had worn to the guild in Zurich. That day, he was the old Jakob, the philosopher.

"Our lives have been, of late, one of suffering, but it is for our good, our benefit. We are learning many things through these times, aren't we?" he said to Priscilla with a faraway look. "We are learning, we are changing. Changing for the better. Our hearts are full, we have many blessings, and many memories, and they fill us to overflowing. Our lives have been rich. I choose to think on the good today."

A little later that morning, he told Priscilla, "I have a strong sense that I should walk into Waldshut and look for Josef this afternoon."

She looked at her father with eyes of love. "Do you want me to go with you, Papa?"

"No, I'm on a mission of sorts, and I'm not sure what it is as yet."

❧

Glad to be outside, Jakob walked, enjoying the weather. He nodded to the Waldshut people he met as he walked. Then Josef came up beside him. "Ah, friend," he said, "I hoped we would meet today."

Jakob replied, "And that we have. What is the news from the Waldshut guild these days?"

"We have missed you there," Josef said.

"I was feeling poorly for a while but I'm better now."

"The two new apprentices are progressing nicely, I understand. They are doing well, using the looms you provided."

"That is very good news." Jakob smiled, his pace a bit slower than Josef's. "Ah. I think my mission is accomplished. Look, up ahead, Josef."

"Johann . . . Johann, wait up," Josef called out.

The mountain man stopped, turned around, and recognized Jakob and Josef. He walked toward them and said, "Hello, friends."

Josef and Jakob looked at each other in surprise at the response.

"Johann, it's good to see you, old friend." Josef placed his hand on Johann's shoulder. "Are you here on business? I don't remember ever seeing you in Waldshut."

"I've come to this village hoping to find you and Jakob. Could we sit and talk for a time?" Johann motioned toward two benches ahead.

Jakob and Josef sat down, and Johann took the bench facing them. Josef leaned toward him and asked, "What's on your mind?"

"It's about our conversation some weeks ago," Johann said.

"When we stopped at your cabin?" Josef said.

"I have given that time much consideration." Looking at Jakob, he said, "First of all, I was rude to you, Jakob, during our first meeting and for that, I want to apologize."

"Apology accepted," Jakob answered.

"Also, I want to say I have taken in much of what you said about Jesus, and I've taken it to heart. It began to ring true for me." Johann peered out toward the mountains and the two men focused intently on him, waiting to hear more.

Johann continued, "Your message has changed me. I've come to realize what confusion I have lived in, and what darkness was in my heart. I saw how cold my heart was, and somehow this Jesus has warmed my heart." He said this with a lightness in his eyes they hadn't seen before.

"My heart had grown harder and harder," he sighed. "So many trials in life." A bit of darkness shadowed his face. "As I thought about my life, the loneliness and bitterness, I didn't like the man I saw. I wanted to change, but how? Then I thought of you both and seeing the peace on you. Some of what you had said came back to me about how you trusted in God, in Jesus. I thought about what I had seen of you, and I considered you to be honest, forthright men. I trusted you, so maybe I could trust this man, this fellow Jesus.

"I thought about the loneliness that had taken over my life. And it came to me that I don't need to be lonely. A bit of a walk and I'm in our little town where my daughter and my grandson reside. What if I forgave my daughter? Long ago, something came between us. I'm not even sure what it was now. If I forgave her and made amends, we would be a family again. So, I have done so. Easy, simple. What took me so long? I see this so clearly from this side. Why didn't I see it before?" Johann said with a wry smile.

"And now we are a family again. Yes, I have come to trust in the Savior." He pointed to his heart. "Maybe I'll even take up prayer or go into the village to take communion from time to time. Even take in some sermons in the little church." He paused. "Well, I don't know about that. To tell you the truth,

I don't enjoy the pastor there. He's boring." He looked at the two men and winked. "I know, you're thinking I'll need to change my opinion of him. I hoped I could find you today to thank you for your effort to help an old man."

They laughed together with Johann and encouraged him. They agreed to meet again and talk more.

"I will take leave of you now and I thank you again." Johann bowed his head to them. They watched as he slowly walked down the street and around the corner to make his way out of the city.

After he was gone, Josef looked at Jakob and chuckled. "I have to say, that was unexpected. I feel like we are marveling at a miracle. I have talked to that man many times about Christ. I had given up. But then you came along, Jakob, and you had the right words for him."

On the walk home to the cabin, Jakob considered his day and how extraordinary it was. When he arrived, he shared with Priscilla the conversation in the village. "I had such a strong sense that I should go into town, Priscilla. I was searching for something, and now I know what it was."

Priscilla saw that look on his face—like he was seeing something others didn't see.

Jakob went on, "Johann was searching, and he found what he was looking for." Then Jakob said, "I'm going to bed, daughter. I believe I have a bit of a fever tonight."

Chapter 37

Travail, tears in secret shed
over hopes that lay as dead

"Is your Papa better today?" Anna asked as she joined Priscilla in the main room of the cabin.

Shaking her head, Pricilla said, "Not really. It's been three days now." Her face reflected her crushed hope. "Yesterday it looked like he was improving. Now I fear that was false hope."

"The herbs aren't helping?"

"I've tried every preparation I could think of. I'm running out of ideas. And he's been delirious for days. Did you hear him singing? It was part of a song we used to sing at our gatherings. It was after you went to bed. He sat up, and in his wavering voice, he sang just a short bit of the song. Then he lay back again."

Later in the evening, when Priscilla was done with supper, she sat by Jakob's bedside, wiping his brow and praying. Her father opened his eyes and said, "I feel I haven't long for this world, dear daughter."

"Don't say such things, Papa."

"It is true though, and it must be said. My regret is I will be leaving you and Anna and the baby. Who will take care of you?"

Priscilla turned away, not wanting her father to see her tears. Her facade of bravery was cracking. She asked herself the same question: *What will we do?*

Later, Priscilla was weary from the long hours. She lay her head down for a moment and fell asleep. "I see Christ in the heavens," her father said, startling her awake. Jakob continued, speaking out strongly, "Jesus looks down upon us with care and love. I see that very clearly, I see it." His voice faded away. But then, he rallied to say, "I see many gathered around His throne from every tribe and tongue, I see Him and He's beautiful, Priscilla. He's so beautiful, it's hard to describe. All those gathered around Him see it also and they bow down, as they should."

Priscilla was fully awake now, awestruck at what her father was saying. "I wish I could see it, Papa."

"Oh, magnify the Lord with me, and let us exalt His name forever."

Another song we sang, she remembered.

He was quiet for a time and then spoke again. "Someday people will be free to believe as we believe. There will be freedom of religion, true freedom." Then he lifted his voice and spoke out strongly, "The Kingdom of this world has become the Kingdom of our Lord and of His Christ, and He will reign forever and ever."

Then he was quiet. She sat with him, holding his hand, and watching him breathe. Finally, he took one last breath, and she knew he was gone.

Chapter 38

With Jakob gone, Priscilla and Anna's lives took on a new rhythm. Much of the household chores fell to Priscilla now. Anna helped now and then, but she was often busy with the baby. Priscilla didn't complain; things were simpler, more basic now. She sometimes yearned for home in Zurich, but she was surprised at how she had adjusted to this new season. One big regret was that her design skills for the tapestry in Zurich were no more. Still, she sometimes worked at the Waldshut guild. Today she planned to walk there.

She stepped out of the cabin into the bright sun, shining golden on the path. Looking down the narrow road, she realized she was beginning to feel more settled in the village. The gatherings were filled with old friends now that more brethren from Zurich were fleeing to Waldshut. It made it feel more like home.

Sometimes William joined the meetings. Her father's opinions about William's intentions came to mind as she walked. She wasn't sure how she felt about him. Perhaps she was too old for marriage—or perhaps not. She puzzled over this as she entered the guild. Wanting to get right to work she sat down and began working the familiar rhythm of the loom. She was surprised at how much comfort this old routine brought to her after she had taken it up again after her father had died. It had been three months since his loss. A loneliness had settled on her. She couldn't shake it and wondered how long she would have to suffer with that feeling. As she sat lost in her thought, she looked up to see someone with children walking toward her. "Katrina!" she exclaimed. "It's been much too long. How are you doing?"

"Anna said we could find you here." Katrina pointed to two of her children. "The little ones and I are here in Waldshut now. My husband will follow. We had to leave the city, Priscilla," she said sadly. "The council was putting pressure on us, with the new baby you know. We didn't want to baptize, so here we are." Katrina sighed. "I was sorry to hear about your father. He was a great man and I admired him so." Katrina continued, "Did you hear about Remy? We got word that he was killed in the peasant wars."

Priscilla's heart sank. "No, we haven't heard that. Oh, not Remy!" She felt the weight of the news, and feared how Anna would feel.

The walk home to the cabin was one of dread. How would Anna react? Priscilla also had come to feel a great sense of affection toward the young man who had been such a part of their lives for a time. Priscilla had noticed that

Anna seemed despondent lately; her only joy was the baby. She hoped this new knowledge wouldn't send Anna deeper into a dark place. As she walked, Priscilla prayed and went over in her mind different herbal combinations she might suggest to Anna.

Priscilla entered the cabin, leaving the door open. It seemed stuffy in the room today. She paused to watch Anna change the baby's clothes and prop her up on the bed. Anna stood back to admire the child. Priscilla did the same. Then she reluctantly turned toward Anna. "Come, sit with me. I have something to tell you."

Once Anna was settled beside her, Priscilla took a deep breath. "I saw Katrina in town." She paused, hoping Anna wouldn't be hurt too much by the news. Then she said slowly, "She said our Zurich friends received word that our friend Remy has been killed in the peasant wars." She let the weight of it settle.

Anna stared at her, shocked. Then she collapsed against Priscilla's shoulder. Priscilla put her arm around Anna and tried her best to comfort her. She was surprised at Anna's level of pain. She hadn't realize she'd cared for Remy that much.

When Anna composed herself, she looked up at Priscilla, tears pooling in her eyes. "Remy was so caring and gentle with me," she said. "He wasn't who I thought he was. He seemed arrogant and haughty at first." She paused, thinking about him. "But he was very tender with me," she said.

"Time will heal, child," Priscilla said softly.

"I don't feel assured of that," Anna replied sadly.

Priscilla saw what she interpreted to be a sense of hope-lessness overtake Anna.

❧

The next day the sun rose bright, and it sparkled on the cabin's windowsill. Priscilla started her walk into Waldshut with the promise of a rewarding day at the guild. She left Anna by herself to attend to the baby. Anna fed the little one, enjoying the quiet of the cabin. After singing a little lullaby to her, she laid the baby on the bed and moved to the table for a small lunch when she was startled by a knock at the door. Answering, she gasped and stepped back. It was Fredrik.

"Are you going to let me in?" he said, boldly walking into the cabin and stopping to look around. Anna stepped behind the table as if it were a barrier of protection. A fear she hadn't felt since leaving Fredrik rose in her. Her entire body tensed, as if she might need to prepare to flee at any moment. She waited, wondering why he was here.

After his inspection of the simply furnished cabin, Fredrik turned to look at her and said, "So this is where you choose to live." His face showed his disdain. "You left my beautiful home for this? And without a word. Why?"

Anna hoped to deflect the question. She knew instinctively that she couldn't control the conversation, but she hoped she could direct it. "So," she said, "how did you find me?"

Fredrik ignored the question, and his voice grew louder. "Why did you leave me? For this?" He threw his arm out wildly. Anna knew him well enough to realize he was growing explosively angry. She was concerned that the volume of his voice would wake the baby.

It was difficult to do, but she moved closer to him. The fear was overwhelming, but she had to protect the baby. She lowered her voice and spoke slowly, "I was afraid of you then, Fredrik, and I'm still afraid." With this, she gained some courage. "You should see yourself. I think anyone would fear you." She looked straight at him then and saw that her effort seemed to calm him. *It's working*, she thought.

He moved closer to her. Looking directly into her eyes, he pulled her into an embrace. A flood of feelings came over her.

Fredrik leaned down to whisper in her ear, "Remember our nights together? Come back to Zurich with me."

She breathed in deeply. His smell, his body next to hers. She remembered how she felt at one time toward him, and she felt confused again. *Was this love? Or something else?*

Then, the baby cried from the bed behind the curtain and Anna's eyes widened with anxiety again.

"What's that?" he said, looking at her, puzzled.

"That's our child," she answered with hope in her eyes.

Fredrik stared in the direction of the cry. He looked at her, his face taking on an expression she couldn't read, and he pulled away from her.

"Our child?"

Anna hurried to pick Barbara up, took her out of the bedroom area, and presented her with pride to Fredrik. "Here she is. You have a baby."

Fredrik stared at the child again, at a loss for words. "A baby, I don't know Anna. I want you to come with me. But a baby? Maybe someone could take care of it here."

"I won't leave without my child, Fredrik . . . our child." She looked on with determination as he considered the situation. "Look at her, Fredrik. She looks like you, just like you."

He stared at the baby for a moment and Anna thought she saw his face soften a little. Frederick turned toward Anna. "All right, we will take it," he said impetuously. "Get your things and let's go."

❧

Chapter 39

Over the hum of her loom, Priscilla caught hints of conversations that were popping up around the room. She had wanted to get some time on the loom before the meeting called for that evening started. The noise of her loom blocked most of the conversation, but as she looked about, she saw those usually bent over their spinning wheels whispering, their heads close together. She heard a word or two . . . something about an army and Prince Ferdinand. It didn't make much sense and she wasn't one for gossip, so she determined to ignore it. But the palpable air of tension in the room was something she couldn't deny. Finally, to her relief, it was time for the meeting and people began migrating toward their chairs or benches in the large main room.

Priscilla took the chair that had been her father's. She'd been given that place of honor since he was gone; the elders had recognized the calling on her life and wanted to continue to honor Jakob.

The meeting started with a song Felix had written. The Zurich people were familiar with it, and it was one the Waldshut members were coming to appreciate. Where was Felix tonight and how did he fare?

Priscilla glanced at the door and saw William hurriedly enter the room, walk directly to Master Hubmaier, and whisper something to him. The master sat up with an expression of concern. Then she watched William walk to his seat. He was coming more regularly these days, which made sense now that all the meetings were shut down in Zurich.

When the singing ended, Master Hubmaier moved to the front of the room with his bible in hand and read a scripture on love and forgiveness. There would be no preaching tonight. The scripture had been read the week before; it was one the group had meditated on over the week and now discussion would begin. The meeting was lively, with comments from those gathered. Priscilla added a comment and asked a question. Master Hubmaier, in his humble way, admitted he did not have an answer for her. He asked what others in the group thought. For that honesty, Priscilla admired him even more. With all this running through her thoughts, Priscilla hadn't noticed that the atmosphere in the room had changed. She looked up to see the master laying down his bible.

"And now I have some news to share. Some very unpleasant news." He glanced around the room and said grimly, "Our brother William has come from Zurich to tell us the council has announced plans to shut down our guild for having what they consider to be illegal religious meetings."

The room erupted with voices clamoring. "How can they do that? How do they have the authority?"

Master Hubmaier put up his hand to quiet the crowd. "And they will be sending a proclamation to order me to appear before them." As reality settled over them, the crowd quieted. Looking around at each other, they became solemn.

Later, after most of the group had left, Balthasar, Priscilla, and William sat together in the empty hall, pondering the gravity of this new decree.

Finally, Balthasar spoke. "Thank you, William, for traveling the distance to bring this news. I'm grateful to you."

William said, "You may want to consider leaving the area, Balthasar. You will be putting yourself in danger by going to Zurich. They will most likely want you to recant. To them we are heretics."

Priscilla noted William's use of *we* and rejoiced that he considered himself one with them. Priscilla leaned toward Balthasar. "Perhaps you should consider William's wisdom in his suggestion of avoiding the council. They can be vicious."

William interrupted. "I have wanted to tell you about an area in Moravia I have been traveling to for several years. They have freedom there to worship as they please. The nobles of the area protect them."

"That is something to consider, brother," Baltasar answered. "But for now, I have made up my mind to speak with the Zurich council. I want to appeal to them to leave the guild open. Our people will suffer without a place to produce their wares. I can't let that happen." He looked at William directly.

"I have another thing I haven't spoken of yet. I didn't want to add to the burdens of the day for the larger group. I have been warned by Prince Ferdinand . . ."

Priscilla broke in, "Ferdinand, the Archduke of Austria?"

"The Archduke sent word that he intends to return the oversight of Waldshut to the Catholics. He has ordered me to give it over to him or he will take it. Have you heard his motto? It's 'Let justice be done, though the world perish.'"

The shock they felt was thick in the room.

Priscilla spoke first, "What does he mean, he will take it?"

Balthasar answered, "He says he will send his armies to take it."

Priscilla shuddered.

Priscilla and William started toward the cabin with this news heavy on their hearts. She wondered if she should tell Anna. Would it be too much for her to bear? At the cabin she bid goodbye to William. But as she opened the door, she immediately knew something was wrong.

"Anna?" Walking to her sleeping area, Priscilla opened the curtain, and asked again, "Anna. Where are you?"

Chapter 40

Two weeks later, William helped Priscilla wrap her cloak around her shoulders. "It's getting dark," he said. "Let me give you a ride to the cabin."

There was no objection on her part. She welcomed his companionship, feeling keenly her new place of isolation. The cabin was too quiet these days, and she didn't want quiet. What she wanted was to hear the baby cooing and watch Anna leaning over the child, speaking softly. That normality was agreeable and cherished. She wished she could return to that time.

As the wagon made its way down the path out of the village and toward the cabin, William said, "Priscilla, I have some news that I believe you will welcome."

Priscilla looked ahead and saw the cabin lighted by the glow of the moon. With anticipation and hope gathering in her heart, she said, "There's the cabin, let's sit on the bench." Arriving at their destination, they each took a seat. She said, "I would ask you in, but I live alone now."

"That's what I wanted to speak to you about. I believe I saw Anna in Zurich."

"What?"

"I believe I saw her sitting outside the priest's house."

Finding it hard to believe Anna would go back to the priest, Priscilla felt stunned. She turned toward William and said, "William, you bring me such consolation." And she smiled for the first time that afternoon. Looking down at her hands folded in her lap, she said, "Anna just disappeared. I was so very worried; it wasn't like her." She looked up at him and said, "It just didn't make sense, William."

"And now you are all alone in this cabin." William looked at her with eyes of compassion. "How do you feel about that?"

She began to pour out her heart in an uncharacteristically open way to him. "Everything has happened so fast, William. It is not my choice to be alone but that's what has come about," she said with resignation, surprised that she trusted him enough to share her deepest thoughts.

William turned to her. "Priscilla, there is something I have in my heart concerning you. I don't like to see you alone here. I see how you are burdened with no man to care for you."

Priscilla looked at William out of the corner of her eye and wondered what he was going to say.

"I want to marry you, Priscilla. I have always admired you, surely you have known that." He scanned her face.

Looking straight ahead, Priscilla tilted her head, thinking about what William had said in the past to her. How could she have been so obtuse? Her father had tried to tell her.

Facing William, she saw something new in his expression, a deep caring. "William, I just don't know what to think of your offer of marriage. I'm older and this isn't something I have given much consideration."

William took her hand. "I hope you will give it more thought. I'm not asking this out of pity or any such emotion. I have thought about it for some time, even before your father passed away. I care deeply for you."

Priscilla heard the sincerity in his voice, yet she was shocked. Marriage to William? She had thought that she was beyond the age of marriage. But it appeared William didn't agree. Perhaps it was out of pity, although he made the point of saying that wasn't the case. She wished her father was here to give her counsel. But reflecting on it, she felt she knew what his answer would be.

"Please just consider it, Priscilla," William said.

The wind howled at Remy's back as if to announce the changing of the season. It compelled him on. He walked the city looking for her. The thought haunted him, *What am I doing? She's not here, I've looked for days. But then . . . wait, wait. . . . Is that her?*

"Jorg, Jorg! Hey, wake up!" Remy shook him hard, trying to wake his friend out of a deep sleep.

Jorg shook his head as if shaking off a dream. He sat straight up in the bed and stared at Remy as if he were seeing an apparition. "Whoa, whoa. What's happening? You're dead!"

Remy laughed. "Jorg, it's me. I'm obviously not dead, right? I'm talking to you. You thought I was a ghost, huh?"

"What are you doing here? They said you were dead," Jorg said slowly, still half asleep. "You're dead, that's what they told us!" He said it again, staring hard at Remy.

"Whoever they were are wrong, I'm not dead!" Remy exclaimed.

"Some of the peasants told us you died in the wars." Jorg rubbed his eyes and looked at Remy again. "You're sure you're not dead?"

"Come on, Jorg, I need you to help me."

"Sure Remy, anything for you. I'm glad you're not . . . you know, dead," Jorg said, rubbing more sleep from his eyes, looking closely at Remy.

"Anna is here in the city, and I need you to help me rescue her from that priest. We'll talk tomorrow and I'll explain everything."

"Remy, what are you talking about? Don't leave me hanging."

"All right, here's the plan. We are going to dress up as monks . . ."

❧

Chapter 41

Remy and Jorg sat on a bench across from the priest's house. They wore their robes. Hoods covered their faces and their heads were bent down. "We'll wait for the priest to leave, then knock on the door," Remy said. "We will pretend we don't know the priest is out. We will say we have an urgent need to talk to him. The cook will surely have to go to market this morning. She'll leave, then we'll look for Anna."

"Are you sure this will work?"

"Of course, it will. It must work," Remy said forcefully, glancing around nervously. They settled in for the long wait.

Jorg, attempting to offer instruction on how to look like a monk, said to Remy, "Remember the *Our Father*?" There was no response. "Remember it?" Jorg began: "Our Father, which art in heaven . . ." He glared at Remy. "Aren't you going to join in?"

Remy stared into the distance with a hard look on his face.

"Remy, why don't you join in?"

"I don't pray," Remy said, still staring straight ahead.

The former monk couldn't imagine that. No prayer. He sat considering that for a while. No conversation passed between them for a time. Then Remy asked, "You used to be a monk, right?"

"Yes, I was."

"Why did you become one?"

"Because I loved God."

"Why did you leave?"

"Because I loved God."

Remy had his eyes trained on the door when the priest come out. "There he is." They continued to bow their heads as they had agreed upon, with their hoods obscuring their faces. They watched him walk out of sight. Then they slowly approached the door and knocked. The cook opened the door and stood in the entry staring at them. She looked from Jorg to Remy and back, saying nothing.

Jorg felt the sweat forming on the back of his neck. He summoned his courage and said, "We are here to see Father Fredrik."

"He is not here," the cook said sourly.

Remy bowed, and with his best monk imitation, said, "We will wait for him, we've come a long way."

Jorg looked at him with surprise.

The cook eyed the pair suspiciously. "You want to see him for what reason?"

"We have our reasons. We have come a long way and will not be turned away. It is vital that we see him," Remy said, matching her stare.

Giving in, she shook her head and let them enter. "Sit there," she said curtly, then walked into the kitchen.

"I didn't think she was going to let us in," whispered Jorg. Remy didn't answer.

The cook came back. "Where did you say you were from?" she said snippily.

"We are brothers from the Saint Lucius monastery near Chur. You have heard of it, I'm sure," Remy said confidently, remembering Jorg's instructions.

She continued giving them a stony glare. "I'm sure I have." She stood for a time longer, glowering at them.

Jorg, feeling nervous, awkwardly fished for something to say. "Brother, it is time for our prayers. Would you please excuse us, cook? We would like to have privacy for our prayer time." He got on his knees and looked at Remy out of the corner of his eye. Remy followed suit with a look of surprise and uncertainty. "Our Father which art in heaven . . ." With that, she left. Jorg looked at Remy. His look said, *I told you so*. Remy ignored him.

The cook abruptly rushed into the room again after they had finished their prayers. "I'm going out. I don't know when Father will return."

"That is all right. We will wait and pray," Jorg said, the confident one this time. She left just as abruptly as she'd come, slamming the door. They sat very still for a time. Just as they were about to get up to begin the search for Anna, cook rushed back through the door. She picked up her egg basket, threw them a disgusted look, and left.

"Such a pleasant person!" Remy whispered. "Let's get going." They rushed to the top of the stairs. Each took one side of the long hallway, opening every door and calling for Anna.

Anna poked her head out of a door down the hall, then quickly stood in the doorway. "Remy, you're alive . . . !"

"Get your things and the baby. You are leaving with us," Remy said hurriedly.

"But why?"

The two moved closer to Anna. Remy said with intensity, "You know you are miserable here. Look me in the eye and tell me you're not,"

"You know he's right, Anna," Jorg said quietly.

"Get your things. We'll get the baby. Where is she?"

Anna pointed to the next room and Jorg ran to get her.

After they'd gathered everything, they hurried to the first-floor library. Anna suggested it would be the safest escape route. Jorg opened the library window. He hurriedly climbed out with the baby. Then Remy climbed through the window. Anna sat on the windowsill and Remy lifted her down, slower than necessary. He drew her close to him. He looked into her eyes and almost kissed her. Anna, feeling shy and uncomfortable, pushed him away. The baby held out her arm toward her mother and started to cry. Anna took her from Jorg. She was about to thank Remy and Jorg when a look of panic crossed her face. She said desperately, "My book, Remy. I can't leave without my book."

"Your book?" Remy looked at her with disbelief.

"Yes. Oh please, Remy," she begged. "It's on the chair next to the desk."

He was about to refuse, but looking into her eyes that were so earnest and needy, he said, "All right." He quickly climbed back through the window, picked up the book, and was ready to leave when Fredrik burst through the door.

Seeing Anna outside the window, Fredrik shouted, "What are you doing, Anna?" And to Remy, "You can't take her!"

"We are taking her, and you have nothing to say about it," Remy shouted back, standing his ground.

"I have everything to say about it. She's mine. I own her," the priest replied.

Jorg, feeling the need to come to Remy's aid, started to climb back into the room. Remy stood before the priest. Glancing over his shoulder he said, "Jorg, I can take care of this." Remy turned toward Fredrik. "You have absolutely nothing to say about this. She is not yours. You have abused her these many years, and you know it. You have no right to her."

Fredrik moved closer to Remy and yelled, "I will not allow you to take her." He looked out the window and said, "You will stay with me, do you hear, Anna!"

A rage arose in Remy, and he, being the more powerful of the two, pinned the priest against the bookshelf with an arm across his chest. With his rock-hard face inches from the priest's, he yelled, "Try to stop me and I will make you regret it."

"I will not let you get away with this," Fredrik said weakly.

Remy saw the look of fear on the priest's face. He knew enough about men to be certain this was an empty threat, and they wouldn't be followed. He pushed hard against Fredrik with one last display of anger, ran for the window and climbed through it. Once outside, Jorg said, "Let's get out of here."

They hurriedly ran the two blocks to where the horse and cart were waiting and started quickly out of the city.

Chapter 42

The trio passed out of the city and away from its tensions. As they rode under the canopy of pines that closely lined the path, their somber mood changed to one of merriment. The celebration started with the behavior of the little horse. She was young and not well trained. Remy, sitting next to Anna on the cart, tried to make the little filly behave, but she had a mind of her own. Anna was the first to notice Remy's failed attempts at keeping the young horse in line. She covered her mouth and turned away, not wanting him to see her laughing. She knew he was one who wanted to be in charge and capable. But in this situation, it looked like the little filly was winning. She was slowing down and dropping her head to feed on the grass along the road. Jorg couldn't resist giving Remy a hard time. "Where are your horse skills, brother?" he said with a loud laugh. They continued on but soon lost interest in pushing the horse.

As they rode along together, Anna and Remy shared stories of their childhoods. It was a healing time for them. Remy laughed more than Anna had ever seen him do. He spoke of his time in the hills around Zurich as a boy, of adventures with his friends, and the antics of the sheep they tended.

The two men took turns, one walking and the other sitting next to Anna in the cart. When Jorg rode with Anna he prayed, sometimes loudly. She found herself enjoying his prayers. They were informal, honest, and from the heart. She felt God's presence again. She and Jorg sang songs together. Remy wasn't happy about this and complained about Jorg's off-key singing. "Let Anna sing, Jorg!" he exclaimed.

When it was time for Jorg to walk again and for Remy to sit beside Anna, they rode along in silence for a time. Then Anna said, seemingly to no one, "I thought I loved him."

"Who, Fredrik?"

"Yes."

Remy flinched. *How could she love that man?*

Anna said, as if she'd heard his thoughts, "He was kind to me at times."

"What happened then?" Remy said, pouting a bit.

"He didn't want the baby," she said bitterly. "It doesn't look right for a priest, you know. I escaped and went to live with the brethren. Jakob and Priscilla welcomed me into their home, I felt safe there and hidden. They are people who have had to hide. Do you know that?"

"Yes, I am aware of that. They also welcomed me."

They rode quietly. Then Remy asked, "Do you believe?"

"I have come to believe. My faith is growing. I have much respect for my friends; they have loved me and taught me about faith and true love." She sighed. "Which I guess I must have forgotten because I went back to Fredrik."

"How did that happen?" Remy was curious now.

"I was alone at the cabin, and suddenly Fredrik appeared there. He was so persuasive, and I suppose I recalled the good memories. It was foolish of me, I know." She looked down at her hands. "In a very short time I was miserable again, just as you said. He was always drunk. Then he began to glare at the baby, and that scared me. After that, I didn't let her out of my sight, I was afraid . . . so afraid. Then you two came and rescued me. I am so grateful," she said, trying to read the look on his face.

Remy, wanting to be honest with Anna, sought for words. He found painful ones and spoke them out. "I have a story also. I killed a man."

"What do you mean? In the peasant wars?"

Remy paused. "No, I killed one of my brothers, my fellow pikemen. I did it in a drunken rage because he took my woman from me." He looked at her, half hoping this made her jealous." We were oath brothers. I lost my temper. It's unforgivable." It was a moment of vulnerability, something he seldom allowed.

"People make mistakes, Remy."

He breathed out.

"They said you were dead, Remy."

"I was wounded and out of the fight for a while. I guess someone got it wrong, because here I am, right?"

Anna smiled and looked away.

From the back of the cart where she had been sleeping, the baby woke and started to cry. Anna said, "I need to feed her. Let's stop so I can get her."

Remy jumped down and gave the reins to Jorg. "It's your turn now."

When Anna was done feeding the baby, Jorg climbed into the cart, and they continued toward Waldshut. Jorg started to sing again, over the objections of Remy. Then Jorg began making loud proclamations. "Someday I will marry! And I will have a cart like this with a horse . . . that obeys . . . and I will have many children and a beautiful wife." Jorg looked out of the corner of his eye toward Remy walking beside the cart. With a sly smile, he began to sing again. From the side of the cart, he heard Remy say, "Stop singing, Jorg!"

"There it is, Waldshut," Remy yelled out, walking ahead of the cart. Jorg and Anna could see the few lights through the tall pines.

"We have arrived at last," Anna said. "The cabin is right there." She pointed to the left, so they wouldn't miss the cabin in the dark. Jorg pulled the horse and cart to a stop in front, hopped down, walked up to the door, and knocked.

Priscilla cautiously opened the door. Peeking out, she said with surprise, "Jorg, what are you doing here?" As she opened the door wide to greet him, he stepped aside and spread his arms out so she could see who was with him. She stood there trying to adjust her eyes to the dark. "Who is it, Jorg?"

"It's me, Priscilla," Anna said, standing beside the cart.

"Anna!" Priscilla cried out as she rushed to Anna's side. Putting her hands on Anna's shoulders, she said, "Anna, what happened to you? I was so frightened, you just disappeared. Oh, I don't care, come here, and let me hug you." After a hug, she looked at Anna in disbelief, and then saw Remy, taking all this in. "Remy, is that you?" Priscilla placed her hand over her mouth. "I can't believe it. Remy!" She stood for a minute in shock. "Let's all go inside. I know you have a tale to tell."

Stories were told, including Jorg's version of the horse that wouldn't obey, with Remy reluctantly admitting his part. Jorg looked at Remy watching Anna and offered to help Priscilla clear the table. Remy leaned over to Anna and whispered in her ear, and she walked outside ahead of him.

Feeling shy, Anna hurried toward the little horse to pet her long neck. Remy slowly closed the cabin door, wanting to savor the moment of being alone with Anna. He stood by the door watching her with the horse. Then he walked close to her and asked, "Are you cold?" He took her in his arms, "Is that better?" he whispered in her ear. He glanced back at the door hoping Jorg would give them a few moments alone. He said, "I want to kiss you. Is that all right?"

Without answering, she closed her eyes and lifted her face up to his. Their lips touched in the tenderest of ways, and they lingered there. Once again, their lips touched. This time it was with a passion that couldn't be denied. It was sudden and deep and all-encompassing; they were carried away and joined together for a moment.

Concerned about what the others might think, Anna said, "I need to go in."

"Must you?" Remy looked at her, disappointed. "I suppose it's late and it's cold out here. Tomorrow then?" he said hopefully.

"Tomorrow," she answered. He kissed her hand and watched her hurry to the door. She turned to look at him.

Then he thought he must catch this moment. He called, "Wait!" He ran up to her coming very close and said, "Marry me!"

"I will, Remy, I will." She kissed him on the cheek and hurried in.

The next morning Anna looked around at the familiar surroundings. She was glad to be safe again. Priscilla turned from the small stove and set a steaming cup of herbal tea before her.

"Thank you, Priscilla. This is very welcome. It got colder as it got later in the day, and we went higher into the hills. I didn't have a proper cloak." Anna smiled. "Remy did his best to keep me warm."

"What a story and a daring rescue on the part of those two."

"I was so glad to see them and so shocked to see Remy."

"What was it like at the priest's house?"

"It was terrible. His cook had quit, and I had all the house to care for. I think that's why he wanted me back. He would yell at me when the baby cried, and I tried my best to keep the baby quiet. That was the hardest part. He was furious with me, Priscilla, most of the time. I couldn't join him in his bed."

Priscilla looked relieved.

"I couldn't go to him; I kept thinking of Remy. Of course, that made him even more enraged. I thought when he saw the child, his child, it would change him. I hoped to awaken something within him, but it didn't happen. I was willing to stay and pretend we were a family, but I saw how things were and I just couldn't pretend any longer. Then I was trapped. What could I do to escape? The next day Remy and Jorg showed up." She paused. "Priscilla, I have something to tell you. Remy asked me to marry him again, and this time I said yes."

"Oh, how wonderful!"

We plan to marry soon. All I've ever wanted was a home and to be in the arms of a man who loved me, and now I have Remy."

Priscilla smiled, pleased with the news. Hearing this awakened something in her own heart. Something of which she was barely conscious, yet it stirred there.

Chapter 43

Priscilla was at the Waldshut guild when it happened. She was working with a young woman who was new at the looms. Her new student, Melisenda, was especially eager to learn the trade. Her mother was a widow and there were five others at home. Melisenda was the oldest, so the burden of caring for the family fell on her shoulders. Still, she embraced the challenge.

Priscilla sat at the loom thinking how her father would be pleased that those in need were benefiting from the old looms.

Her young student greeted Priscilla with a smile. "Good day, Master Priscilla."

Amused by the greeting, Priscilla replied, "I'm not sure that title belongs to such as I."

The peasant girl was embarrassed. "Please forgive me, ma'am. What should I call you?"

"Just Priscilla will do. You sit here, and let's see what progress you have made on the loom." She made room for her student.

Instruction started and Priscilla was happy to see Melisenda's skills had grown in a short time. "At this rate, we will have you working on your own very soon."

"Will I continue to work at this loom?"

"You should stay with this one. Each loom has its own peculiarities, so until you get more experience use this one."

"Thank you, Priscilla. I am so grateful to you and your father for this. I'll never forget you."

Just then, they were interrupted by a commotion in the other room. It started with a mild argument but soon there was shouting. Some of the voices they recognized as those who worked on the looms; other voices were of the women who worked at the spinning wheels. Melisenda looked at Priscilla, wide-eyed. They stepped away from their looms. Priscilla started toward the conflict with Melisenda following. They stopped at the door and watched as one man was forcefully pulling a woman away from her spinning wheel while others yelled at him.

Priscilla recognized some of the council members from Zurich. *They have followed us here*, she thought, *and now peaceful Waldshut will suffer*. The two of them continued to watch the struggle, and Priscilla felt Melisenda grow more anxious.

Through the ruckus, one of the young men said, "Why are you doing this?" He repeated it twice.

"We told you when we arrived that you are holding illegal religious meetings here and it will have to stop."

In the confusion, Priscilla hadn't recognized him, but focusing on his voice she realized it was Bruno Heinrich, the magistrate from Zurich that had caused her and her father such pain. Yet she no longer felt the same fear and anger toward him from earlier. She was stronger, braver now. But there wasn't much time to consider the changes in her heart as the men, including the magistrate, moved toward her room. She and her student stepped aside while they tramped into their area.

The magistrate turned toward Priscilla. He growled, "Is this where you work?" Priscilla said nothing. "Bring the sledgehammer," he said to one of the men. They watched as the looms were broken up and turned into useless piles. Knowing Melisenda's dreams were crushed, Priscilla put her arm around her and held her while she cried.

The next day it was announced that the guild was to be closed permanently and some of the leaders would be fined. This was the beginning of many battles and disagreements among the Waldshut brethren. They began to turn against each other. Hubmaier was criticized by some for combining worship with the workings of the guild. The peasants were especially vocal, as they were the ones most affected, with their livelihoods destroyed.

"This one event has set off a firestone of disagreements amongst us," Master Hubmaier said with dismay as he sat discouraged at the table in his home. He was surrounded by some of the elders of their community, and Priscilla had also been invited. He continued, "This is to me the most damaging aspect of this conflict, the fissures in our relationships. Do the people blame me?"

"It's not your fault, Master Hubmaier, the peasants are blaming every one of us," one of the elders said. "Today it is you, tomorrow it is me or someone else."

Another elder added, "It's not just the peasants. There are wild stories flying around the group—gossip, and other madness."

"That's why I've called you together today. I need your wisdom and I need your prayers. I have to tell you that they have summoned me to Zurich." There was a common gasp. "Tomorrow, I leave to what I don't know. Does anyone? Only God." He looked at the elders and Priscilla. "Pray with me tonight, friends."

Later in the month, William helped Priscilla into his cart, hopped up beside her, and took the reins. This had become a welcome habit for them. Whenever William was in town, he saw that Priscilla got home safely from faith meetings. "Are you back from your travels?" she asked him.

"I had a very strong feeling that I needed to come to Waldshut. I've been in Moravia this month. What's going on here? There is a different atmosphere in the town, and I see the guild is shut down."

"The council has summoned Balthasar to Zurich. He's been gone since the guild was shut down. Not a word from him."

With a look of concern, William said, "I'll travel to Zurich then, to see what has happened there."

"Do you still have a house there?"

"I have closed it down. I no longer feel welcome in Zurich. I have offended the council with my support of you and the others." William turned to face her. "I'm moving to Moravia, Priscilla. My business is there, and it just makes sense." William looked at her as if to send an appeal. He ended with, "There is freedom there."

"That is what I've been trying to convince our group," she said. "I want them to at least discuss the possibility, but there is so much chaos and upheaval after the closing of the guild. And some of the men complain strongly about the place I've been given in the fellowship. They refuse my input. Especially now that Balthasar is missing from the meetings. He always supported me against those who criticized me."

William was taken aback. "They don't recognize your gifts," he declared. "God has given you those abilities. You are a good teacher, and you have a God-given gift of leadership."

"Thank you, William. You are a great encouragement to me, and you always have been."

"You know how I feel about you, Priscilla." He looked at her again. "And yet you won't marry me," he said with amused tenderness.

She surprised herself by saying, "Perhaps I'm closer to a decision."

❧

Chapter 44

"They are holding Balthasar at the Wellenberg prison," William said, hurrying in the door.

Priscilla drew in a breath. "The prison where they hold heretics. On what charges?"

"They demand that he recant."

Priscilla sank into a chair. "Why did he go? Why did he put himself in that position? He wouldn't listen to the counsel of the elders. They warned him . . . I warned him. I told him the Zurich council is not amenable."

William spoke with resignation, "That's just Balthasar."

"He had hopes of reconciliation, didn't he? Like my father. And he wanted to speak to the needs of the peasants."

William agreed. He said, "Let's go into the village and talk to some of the brothers."

"I need to finish up a few things in the kitchen." Priscilla put away the meat and dishes. "I'm done, let's walk," she said.

"No need to walk, I have my new wagon. We will ride."

Priscilla closed the cabin and went out to see the wagon. She stood admiring it. "It is huge. And you've gotten new horses."

"I needed the new wagon and the horses. As I said, I'm moving everything to Moravia. There is nothing here for us anymore." He emphasized *us* and looked at her as if to say, *Go with me.*

"I believe that's our only hope," Priscilla said. "We need to persuade the others."

After helping her onto the seat of the wagon, William frowned. "What if we cannot reason with the people? There seem to be many objections to the move."

She sighed again. "We must try. We should call a meeting of the believers."

Standing before the elders that evening as they met in one of their homes, Priscilla said, "Decisions need to be made immediately. William and I have been discussing this; time is running out."

The elders nodded. "We are all aligned with you now, Priscilla," Thomas, one of the elders, said. "We are convinced that a move to Moravia will be best for us . . . but what about the others?

"I believe we can change their minds," Priscilla said. "They need assurance that the plan is workable. We will need to gain the people's confidence in this and bring them to reason. It is understandable that our friends don't want to pick up their homes and move again to a new and unfamiliar area. I understand their fears. Many of those from Zurich have just settled in Waldshut. We had hoped for peace and safety here, but it has not turned out as we wished."

"Let us continue to make this a matter for prayer. And we will call for all to meet tomorrow night," Thomas announced.

The next night, standing before those assembled, Priscilla noticed some in the crowd appeared agitated. The atmosphere was tense, and she hoped the agitators wouldn't influence the others.

Priscilla started, "Dear brothers and sisters, today we gather to consider our future. My hope is you will give much thought to this presentation. Think on it, and most importantly, pray on it. What do you want for your children? Do you want freedom? I believe that we all in our hearts long for freedom. Do you agree with me on this?" Most of the people voiced their agreement. She looked at the agitators and saw she had not yet won them over. She knew some of the peasants still had on their minds the treatment by the overlords and the fact that their livelihoods had been stolen from them. She felt the pain in the room.

"The times have been hard for many of us. Some in this room know, others not, but the guild my father built in Zurich was taken from us, as was our home. I know the pain. Please know I am one with you. I, too, have suffered. I ask this group again, what is our future? If we stay here in Switzerland, will we have the freedom to worship in peace? Will we have the freedom to not baptize our babies? Remember, we are con-sidered heretics here. What will that mean for the future?"

She noted the mood of the room was changing; the crowd had become more somber. "And we have been told the Austrian army is threatening to move on our village to take it back for the Catholics."

Priscilla's student, Melisenda, stood up. She said, "What do you suggest, Priscilla?"

"Is there a place of freedom for us? Yes. Our friend here, William, will explain more about that when I finish. There is a Lord in Moravia who holds our views on faith. He is Moravian nobility by the name Leonhard von Liechtenstein. He knows about our group, and he has agreed to provide a temporary place for us to gather on his estate until we can make further plans."

Someone from the crowd yelled out, "An overlord that wants to help us? Hard to believe."

Priscilla recognized him as one of the agitators. She said, "He is a friend to us. William, please come forward and give us more information." Priscilla looked out over the group, remembering that some of the wild gossip that had gone about the community was focused on William. But today as he walked forward, she was pleased to see the people were ready to hear him out.

"Yes, von Liechtenstein is a friend. I have personally talked with him. He is a strong believer and will be an ally and protector for us. I have also talked with some of the other believers in the area. They tell me the weavers in our group would be welcomed." After this information, there was a hum of conversation in the room. "We see no future here and Priscilla has made a compelling case for why that is. Therefore, our plan is to start for Moravia in two days," William concluded.

One of the agitators called out from the crowd: "How can you travel? It will be impossible this time of year." This further riled the crowd up.

"I have traveled to Moravia on several trips this time of the year. I know the route well. And I want to say that I no longer feel safe or wanted in Switzerland. I long to live in a place that welcomes freedom of conviction, and I believe we will find it there. It is my hope that all of you will join us." William stepped away.

Thomas stood before the brethren. "This seems to me to be a good, workable plan. My question is, should we wait to hear from Master Hubmaier?"

"I am here."

The crowd gasped. Recognizing their leader, they clapped and cheered. The master left his seat in the back where he had been quietly waiting and walked to the front of the room. He said, "I cannot begin to explain how I am back in your presence again. I did not expect to be here, but our Lord had other ideas and I am free, as of yesterday." The crowd cheered again. He held up his hands to quiet them and said, "I am now convinced it is imperative that we leave this area as soon as possible." The people listened intently. "Not only are we under pressure from those in Zurich, but it is a fact that the Austrian army moves toward our city."

Someone in the crowd called out, "Why does the army care about our sleepy village?"

"Remember, at one time we were a strong Catholic holding. The Austrian prince and I have had disagreements in the past, and now he has decided to take back Waldshut."

"What about the peasant armies surrounding the village?" someone called out.

"I do not have confidence that the peasants will protect us this time . . . not against the mighty Austrian army. We need to move out. From what Priscilla and William report, we will be welcome in Moravia. You are free to go as your conscience speaks to you. I want you to know that I am making plans to leave the day after tomorrow. Please join us, as you will. William is prepared to guide us, as he has said, and I believe him to be an able and honorable man. It is my hope Moravia will be to us a Promised Land."

❧

"I wish I could go with you, Priscilla," Anna said. "But I know Remy wouldn't want to leave Switzerland. His heart is still with the peasants."

"And he is a good husband to you, isn't he? I have seen how he looks at you," Priscilla said.

"Yes, he is good and caring, and you have seen how he loves my Barbara, like his own child."

"Yes, how remarkable it is. I know that God brought you together, but I am concerned with you staying here. Will you be safe?"

"My Remy will protect me."

"Yes, he will. He is, after all, a soldier."

"I have to go, my family will be looking for me," Anna said with pride. "Priscilla, I finally have a family that I can call my own."

"I am so very happy for you, Anna. I'll walk you to the door." Opening the door she said, "Hurry on now, sweet daughter." Priscilla stood outside as Anna turned and waved. Priscilla thought with sadness that she would never see her Anna again.

Then her thoughts floated to the next day. She imagined what it would be like watching the new team of horses prancing around the bend and stopping in front of the little cabin. She smiled at how beautiful they were and how proud William was of them. Then she imagined William and how he would greet her. She could hear him say, 'Good morning, sister.' She was surprised at the level of excitement she felt at imagining this, and she knew it wasn't the majestic new horses. It was William himself, his voice, and his presence. She wondered at it.

Chapter 45

Look up, look up to the hills afar

William leaned against the cabin that morning, waiting for the others to come so they could start their journey together. As he watched the sun make its full appearance, his glance went to Priscilla. She sat on the wagon, her back straight and her head held high. *She's so regal,* he thought in admiration.

William mused over their story and what he had been told about how the fire had started for the Brotherhood, with Priscilla seeing Felix preach in the square that day. He'd heard the story many times and could easily picture it: Felix and his bold testimony, how he didn't back down when the council came against them. He knew Priscilla suffered a time of much fear, and he felt a surge of protectiveness for her. He remembered the stories of the prayer meeting and regretted that he hadn't been there, although he felt as if he had experienced it himself. He considered his journey and how surprised he had been that it brought him to join himself to this group.

And Priscilla . . . how he hoped that one day she would agree to marry him, although he wasn't certain he was worthy of her. He glanced her way again, watching the wind blow the curls around her beautiful face. She turned toward him as if she had heard his thoughts, and he nodded toward her. He wanted to share a life with her, to be her mate, to protect her and to hold her in his arms. The thought of that coursed through him. Yes, he wanted to hold her forever if she would have him.

He approached the wagon and carefully checked the horses, the harness, and the rest of the gear one last time. "They are taking longer than I expected," he said as he climbed into the wagon, settling in beside Priscilla.

"I expect the sun will be dancing before us on our journey."

"You are poetic today, sister." He paused. "Is it hard leaving, Priscilla?"

"It was very hard leaving Zurich when we did. We loved our life there, but then there was that still small voice that called us on. My father always said we are all actors in this story of Christ, and we played our part, both there and here." She looked into the distance, considering this. "And now there will be more to the story."

"Do you think Moravia will be the Promised Land as we have hoped?"

"I believe it will be a home for the community and I believe we will be happy there."

They both looked down the road as if imagining the new life.

William turned toward her. "And what about you and me?"

"We will marry there."

He looked at her with astonishment. It took his breath away. "Sister, you never cease to amaze me." Recovering from his surprise, William said, "How did you come to make this decision?"

"Last night. It was then I knew it was right and that we should make our home together. As long as we are together, we will be happy indeed."

William picked up her hand that rested on the wagon seat and gently kissed her fingers, looking into her eyes.

She smiled at him and turned her eyes toward the bend in the road. "There they are." They waited until the group had assembled, and then William picked up the reins. Before guiding the horses out onto the path, he stood, looked back at those behind him, raised his fist, and shouted, "To the Promised Land!"

END

❧

Author's Notes

This book has been a labor of love. It celebrates the brave people who came before us—those who fought for the freedoms we now enjoy: freedom to worship as we choose, and separation of church and state. Researching this project was difficult at times. Some information I found was contradictory. I worked with what I found and have tried my best to keep the history intact while building the storyline.

Readers will want to know what part of this book of historical fiction is based on fact. Here are some answers to questions that may arise.

Are any of the characters real historical figures?
Yes. Felix Manz (whose last name I found several spellings of), Conrad Grebel, his wife Barbara and daughter Issabella, Jorg Blaurock, Balthasar Hubmaier, and Huldrich Zwingli. There was a magistrate in Zurich at the time, but I was unable to find a name. His part in the story is my creation.

Huldrich Zwingli was considered the Swiss reformer. Originally a Catholic priest at the Gross Muenster, he came under the teaching of Martin Luther. He was a great intellectual and debater, and in 1520 he secured permission from the Zurich City Council to preach what he called "the true divine scriptures." These sermons stirred a revolt against the previous Catholic teaching and initiated the Swiss Reformation. His chief difference with the Anabaptists was his belief that the church is subservient to the government and the practice of infant baptism must continue.

Felix Manz was born the son of a Catholic canon who had served at the Gross Muenster church before Zwingli served as "the people's priest" there. He was given a liberal education with a thorough knowledge of Hebrew, Greek, and Latin. After his death, he left a written testimony of his faith in an eighteen-stanza hymn that is still used by the Amish.

Conrad Grebel was the son of a prominent iron merchant. As a student, he studied with a scholarship at the University of Paris given to him by the King of France. A university in Ontario, Canada, established by the Mennonites, has been named for Grebel.

Jorg Blaurock had been a monk at Chur Monastery. After leaving the monastery he traveled to Zurich. He was arrested before Felix's death sentence, whipped with rods, and expelled from the city.

Balthasar Hubmaier had indeed baptized the majority of Waldshut's city council. Also, he had baptized hundreds of citizens in defiance of the militant overlords who influenced this part of the country. He was, at one time, a priest.

What happened to the characters after the story ended?
In December 1525, Balthasar Hubmaier and his followers left the town of Waldshut. Afterward, it was conquered by the Catholic Austrian troops. Upon moving to Moravia, the brethren were protected by the nobles and Lord von Lichtenstein. They later came to be called the Swiss brethren.

In 1526, Conrad Grebel, Felix Manz, and Jorg Blaurock were sentenced to life in prison after the Zurich council introduced the death penalty for "rebaptism." In May or June of that year, Conrad Grebel died of the plague while in prison. By an act of clemency, Felix Manz and Jorg Blaurock were released from prison.

However, in January 1527, Manz became the first martyr of this group. He was executed—thrown into the river Limmat and drowned.

Jorg Blaurock continued to preach in the outlying towns around the city for years. He was later martyred by being burned at the stake in 1529.

Huldrich Zwingi died in 1531 on the battlefield, fighting against the Austrian Catholic armies.

Balthasar Hubmaier was martyred in 1528.

Did the women have a strong voice in this movement?
Yes. One example of that voice was seen in April 1525. Zurich authorities sent an official to collect fines from those who were rebaptized. He encountered a group of very angry women. The wife of one of the locals refused to pay her fine and gave the official a tongue-lashing. One source said that women were

given complete equality, even to the point of being allowed to preach. My research said the reforming ideas were often communicated by women around the spinning wheel. Also, women were jailed as well as the men.

What present day religious groups are descended from the Anabaptists?

Direct descendants would be, as far as I know, the Amish, Mennonites, Hutterites, and the Bruderhof. There were other likeminded groups in other parts of Europe, particularly England. They followed similar paths and were also persecuted.

What brought on the peasant wars?

The sixteenth century was a time of great upheaval in Europe. In 1524 the peasants in Germany went to war against the overlords they served, fighting over a variety of grievances. Although the fighting started in Germany, it ended up spreading to other parts of the continent.

Another aspect of the upheaval was the armies of the Holy Roman Empire attempting to take back land from the Protestants. Zwingli lost his life in one of those battles. It seems Luther's message stirred the storm of the peasants. It was a message that the common man and woman should have a voice in how they chose to worship and how they chose to live.

How widespread was infant baptism?

It was the norm throughout Europe. For more than a millennium, everyone living in Europe was assumed to be Christian by right of birth and baptism. This was symbolized by the practice of baptizing infants.

What is the source of the poetry used?
The lines of the poems at the beginning of the chapters and in the text were by Amy Carmichael, a British woman who lived in India in the early twentieth century. She opened orphanages to rescue young girls from what we would today call human trafficking. All the poetry is taken from Miss Carmichael's book, *Toward Jerusalem.*

The Anabaptist movement exalted the common man and woman and I celebrate that. It began with the elite but became a movement of the people. Quoting from a book by Eberhard Arnold called *The Early Anabaptists*: "Love was the hallmark of their faith. It was their whole being. This was borne out by all their songs and confessions and by the records of their martyrdoms."

This author believes it is the ideas and longings that began to form in the hearts of these groups that have become the basis for our democratic republic. These ideas of freedom have circled the globe. Freedom is the longing of the human heart.

About the Author

Melissa Dugan and her husband Rodney share three children and three grandchildren. They live in Iowa on a quiet street populated by kind people. Melissa is a lover of a well-written story and a long walk, preferably down a path that curves through the woods.